Front cover design by Chocolate Chip Media (http://www.chocolatechipdesign.co.uk/).

Note for Librarians: A cataloguing record for this book is available from Library and Archives Canada at www.collectionscanada.ca/amicus/index-e.html
ISBN 1-4120-7851-2

Trafford's print shop runs on "green energy" from solar, wind and other environmentally-friendly power sources.

Offices in Canada, USA, Ireland and UK
This book was published *on-demand* in cooperation with Trafford Publishing. On-demand publishing is a unique process and service of making a book available for retail sale to the public taking advantage of on-demand manufacturing and Internet marketing. On-demand publishing includes promotions, retail sales, manufacturing, order fulfilment, accounting and collecting royalties on behalf of the author.

Book sales for North America and international:
Trafford Publishing, 6E–2333 Government St.,
Victoria, BC V8T 4P4 CANADA
phone 250 383 6864 (toll-free 1 888 232 4444)
fax 250 383 6804; email to orders@trafford.com
Book sales in Europe:
Trafford Publishing (UK) Limited, 9 Park End Street, 2nd Floor
Oxford, UK OX1 1HH UNITED KINGDOM
phone 44 (0)1865 722 113 (local rate 0845 230 9601)
facsimile 44 (0)1865 722 868; info.uk@trafford.com
Order online at:
trafford.com/05-2749

10 9 8 7 6 5 4 3 2

Dedications

There are many people I'd like to thank for making this fascimile of the contents of my mind possible. There really are too many people to list here, and I know no one reads this bit anyway so I'll make it short.

I'd like to thank my mum and dad for allowing me free reign with my imagination as a kid!

I'd like to thank my mates back-home in Manchester, and those in Bristol :- I'm sure the nights-out we used to have provided inspiration for this book... You know who you are: Dom, Simon, James, Mike, Andy, Chris, Dave, Gregor, Steve, Mark, Paul and others; thanks for putting-up with the txt's!

Thanks to John Sherbourne for listening to my silly ideas and then reading through it all; more than once! Any errors in this final version you can blame him! (only joking John!).

Thanks to Steve Higgins for taking my original cover design and turning it into something that looked good!

A special dedication must go to Zaf 39 ⁺ . A man of great wisdom, understanding and humour, may he stand forever proud and may he find that which he seeks.

To you all, Chôhk dii, and thanks for all the Beer!!

Preface

This book has come about as homage to those 'Magical' Grimoires of the past which have, though utterly fake and, in some cases ridiculous, been issued upon the general public with great mystery and enthused enthusiasm.

This book was constructed in the spirit of all those that came before, and was constructed for all those people who are not too proud to have a bit of a laugh at themselves.

Although some parts of this book may seem offensive to some people, this wasn't the intended intention… If you are easily offended, then with the greatest respect you shouldn't be buying a book purported to provide 'Evocations for Heme and his minions; The Roids'. Indeed, amongst those people of a sensitive inclination the very title 'The Book of the Roid' should keep you away.

But for those people game or brave enough to venture through these pages I hope you will find satisfaction herein.

And here is a note of caution. Although this book is completely made up, fabricated, false, the ideas presented herein do, in a roundabout way follow the ideas of current magical practise. Therefore I don't advise undertaking any of the rituals herein even for a laugh, without due consideration. If you implant a seed firmly enough within the mind, it will grow. And whilst I can't guarantee the appearance of Heme or any of the Roids (greater or lesser Roids), the mind can play tricks….

As a last piece of advice, if you start to have unnatural feelings for tomatoes, or unsavoury

ideas about painting your front room in a garish
shade of red, see a doctor!

You Have Been Warned!

**"And when the Valley runs Red with the blood of the
Abused, then will Heme realise that the Seed of the
Sons of Adam is Strong no more. And he shall awaken
from his deep slumber, and Mother Earth will weep
once more for her Children"** Joseph. 41.

Introduction

This script was chanced upon during a friend's travels to ancient East Asia. The friend shall, for the purposes of our discussions, be called Joseph.

My friend was a learned person who had during his lifetime frequented much of the Earth upon which we live. He had been to America, travelled around Europe, dined with the tribes of Africa, climbed the ancient temples of the Maya and had also spent a week in Grimsby.

My friend, bored with his current job decided to pack up and leave for mysterious Egypt; land of the Pharaohs, home of the Pyramids and playground for a number of extremist terrorist groups.

He went along with a 'guided' group and toured the many great sites Egypt has to offer. However, due to a groping 'accident' that went horribly wrong, Joseph was expelled from the group. He was left to ponder by himself for the next week of the holiday.

During his pondering he visited an old Egyptian market. Amid the camel-hides, odd-shaped edibles and dusty trinkets he came across a book. This was purely by chance, for Joseph was often too drunk to read.

Whilst he was pondering about amongst the stalls, smoking his pipe of pot, his stash fell-out of his pocket. He stooped to gather his fallen stash of Hashesh and noticed a book. He noticed the book largely because his stash fell onto it.

The book caught his eye with its red-raw cover, a

cover that seemed to be made of living skin (later found to be sewn together from a thousand dried-out haemorrhoids). As if drawn to the book by some unnatural force, Joseph held it aloft and enquired to the stallholder as to the price required for such a red item. The stallholder, a wisened old man, his face half-obscured by a blackened cowl, started to laugh. Joseph took a large puff of his pipe and, when the smoke had cleared the stall had disappeared….

As Joseph started to leave he heard shouting behind him. He turned to find the stall hadn't disappeared; he was just facing the wrong direction… Joseph had been warned before about his drug taking….. He settled with the old man then made plans to come home.

Upon his return to the UK Joseph called and told me of the book and of his wonderful journey. He also wanted me to bail him from jail (a groping 'accident' on the plane had gone horribly wrong….).

After the bailing he showed me his book. My goodness it was red.

It felt soft to the touch, warmly. It attracted but repelled at the same time. It felt like an arse.

I was able to glimpse the book in its raw form, a form which has now vanished (this book is a copy of Joseph's translation). In its original, the text seemed to be of Arabic descent and Joseph set about translating it.

Joseph kept in contact during his translation of the document. He seemed very excited about his progress on the matter. However, after two months of constant contact his calls and letters ceased.

After a further month of non-correspondence from Joseph I informed the Police. They went round to Josephs house and found him dead. His death was a suicide, they said. He'd bled to death from his anus, largely because he'd stuck a kitchen-knife up there. Repeatedly.

Sodomy of the self leading to fatal anal butchery.

Upon the walls of his fridge were written the words "TOM ART THOU" and upon his bedroom wall was scrawled "HEME COMETH". Both writings seemed to be the combined effort of blood and excrement, the latter substance providing the viscous necessary for prolonged 'sticking'.

Herein lies my first warning about the use of this book. It should not be read in jest. Within these pages lie the rituals to evoke a great sleeping evil. I urge caution to anyone fool hardy enough to practise these blackened-arts within; Joseph fell victim to the book, as must have many before him.

I myself have read the book and, although not evoking any of the primal forces within, I too have been affected by these dark powers. I constantly have nightmares about vague shapes, all a maddening shade of red. Since producing this copy of Josephs work I have had many, many stomach upsets and I seem to be developing a fetish for tomatoes too.

However, even though the book is dangerous I feel it necessary to present it here to you, the readers. The book details an ancient evil, one that has already began to stir. To fight this evil we must first understand it, hence the book offers both evocations and exorcisms. We, the people of Earth must be ready for the time whence this evil shall awaken.

Please note that wherever Joseph had made a

personal note in the margins of his translation, I have also included it for completeness.

May the force [of good] be with you, as you undertake this most perilous journey into the darkest pits of oneself.

"And HEME shall ride forth upon the back of his hairy green turtle, and all shall burn in the wake of his minions. Kings and peasants; the Roids are no discriminator of class. All shall be cast into the period of The Ever Lasting Stance". Joseph. 41

A Note About The Author

I feel it is necessary here to speculate about the possible origins of the original script, and also as to its possible author. The name inscribed upon the script, but in handwriting that differed from the main-body of text, reads "AL AZZABIGUN".

AL AZZABIGUN (whom shall be referred to from now on as AA) was, purportedly an ancient Arab priest who was disgraced from the priesthood for some groping 'accident' [gone horribly wrong] with a bunch of Nuns and a soiled copy of the 'Karma Sutra'. And for flashing his cock at a monkey.

AA wasn't always a priest. He started life as a simple milkman, delivering milk to his community. He soon got kicked out of this job however following a particularly nasty incident involving a milk bottle, a loaf of bread and some accidental groping. Following his disgraceful retirement from the milk-catering trade he joined the priesthood.

AA spent his life as a priest researching ancient Arabic folklores and hidden manuscripts. It appears that his dealings with this ancient knowledge caused him to compile a grimoire to warn of the forces that he encountered. He also seemed a bit spiteful at his rejection at the hands of the Nuns. Apparently they were all Lesbians. Even the habited monkey…

We can only speculate as to AA's country of origin, but I can say without a doubt that he came from a place which is now (or what once was) Modern Iraq.

The stallholder told this to Joseph, and he told me. And thus to you, my readers, have I now passed-on the origins of AL AZZABIGUN.

The manuscript reached my hands split into three distinct books. Whether this split was caused by Joseph, AA, or an even more sinister force no one shall ever know… The split was caused by Joseph though. He told me.

Book 0 is an introduction of sorts and touches on how the Universe came into being, how it will end, how the Roids came to be and what the future may hold for us mostly-naked primates.

Book 1 is a roster of sorts; it gives details of all the Greater Roids and also of their place of residence. Scary stuff….

Book 2 is the Book of Calling. This is where things get really red. Using the knowledge gained from Books 0 & 1, you should feel well prepared for the Evocation rituals given here. Beware, this chapter is truly shit-your-pants scary. It is also the chapter where both AA and Joseph descend into complete madness.

I have included my own addition to the manuscript: Book 3. This book contains any additional notes and diagrams that Joseph made during his translation. Book 3 is possibly the worst of this manuscript, as Joseph has truly descended into the abyss at this point. Read with caution.

Formatting of the chapters within these Books was carried-out by myself, for ease of reading.

AA starts the manuscript with a quick introduction and a description of his own folly into the realm of the Roid. However, towards the end of the manuscript the strain on AA is plain to see [read]. He appears to be driven mad by his own scripture and one can only speculate upon whatever fate befell him. And again I must here issue a warning to potential practitioners of this text: It is dangerous. You must be strong in mind and in arse to carry-through these ceremonies with any degree approaching success.

We don't know how poor AA met his end. Perhaps like Joseph, in a pool of savaged-arse blood. There are rumours that AA is still alive, hidden in a cave somewhere along the border of modern Pakistan… However he'd be really old by now, and I'm sure he'd be experiencing problems with his kidneys amongst other things.

Let us assume that AA is dead, for no one could live as long as the age of the original manuscript. One thing is certain; the original book may well have absorbed AA's aura, for it did smell a bit (and, as mentioned previously it did feel somewhat like an arse).

The madness suffered by poor AA can be compared to that suffered by my friend, Joseph. That this book contains evil there is no doubt. However, for the sake of mankind, and for the sake of the monkey we must learn the knowledge of the Roid, so that we can defeat the evil when it chooses to emerge. Be wary at all times, for the Roids do not wait on etiquette, for they beeth the keepers of Red, and thy breathers of Fire.

On a final note as to the content of the manuscript; it seems to be written by a madman, a person wavering on the edge of his mind and the Abyss beyond. However it does appear through its controversy to be carrying a secret message to us all. To those people offended by the material carried herein, why did you buy it? Ching Ching goes the cash register of life…

A Note Upon On The Age Of The Manuscript

Within this chapter I shall speculate upon the age of this most-rightly feared manuscript. I shall provide evidence to backup my claims, and although at first the evidence may appear flaky, made-up and fragmented even…, further investigation will prove that I am right and that you are wrong.

Firstly, the original manuscript was written in Arabic (of sorts), which is a very old language indeed.

Secondly, AA, though his age wasn't given specifically must have lived a very long time ago indeed, and he himself must have been of quite some age (to have lived all the adventures he had lived).

Thirdly, the book was purchased in Egypt. Egypt is very, very old. In fact there are only one or two Pharaohs alive today, which just shows how old it is. Because the manuscript was purchased within a place of this antiquity, it goes without saying that it too must be very old.

Any lingering doubts as to the age of this document can be resolved by the font used. The original translation (provided by Joseph) was compiled in a really old-looking Gothic-type font. For ease of reading, I had to translate this into a modern-English-looking font. However, I have still left in some remains of the original font used during translation. Flick-through the pages of this tome and find those fonts and look at them, feel their age with your eyes. The font proves the book is really, really old. Older [probably] than most of your mums. Though it's not older than Steve's mum. His mum is old. Really old. His mum is known as the Spider Witch, because of what's kept in her bush.

·

Hail the Roid.

LIBER 0 :: HISTORY OF OUR BEING

Introduction

This is a record of all that I have done and all that I have seen.

I used to be an Executive Supplier of Milk Engineer, or an ESME. I was famed throughout my land for my extra creamy milk products. I used to provide cow milk, sheep milk, goat milk, rat milk, cat milk, chicken milk, spider milk and man milk. The head on my milk was the creamiest in all the land. I was the best Goddamn ESME in the whole country.

Every day during my rounds women would raise their Index and outward-joining fingers in an inverted triangle gesture. I do not know truly what this meant, though I think that it could only mean they wanted me to stand on their floored shoulders and perform a vertical shuffle. Even the men started giving me this gesture, which I found a bit disturbing.

One day I tried to progress this love-gesture and found, to my horror that this was not the meaning of the gesture at all! They didn't want me at all. Fucking teases. However I had the last laugh. I strapped an empty bottle to my thigh and cut a hole in my dress-pocket. I always delivered the milk with a smile, and became quite good at carrying my milk with a single hand. This was one of the reasons the company sacked me. That and an accident with a loaf of bread.

But that is all in the past. Alas I have changed.

I am, or was a proud member of the priesthood but I abused my position, and some Nuns, and a Monkey, thus disgracing both myself and my Order. I turned

away from the path of the good and wandered down the
lonely road of evil until it ceased at the foot of a
cave within a forested valley set upon my arse.
I found my arse hidden away within the collected
myths and legends of my order; it was a legend
willingly forgotten by many due to its utter
hideousness.

I spent many years researching this legend, sifting
through countless age-worn manuscripts and avoiding
contact with Nuns. And monkeys.

Finally I came across a weather-beaten tome
disguised as a book of pleasure. As I prepared for
self-pleasure, silken hankies in abundance, the tome
fell onto the toilet-cubicle floor and landed not
upon a page of sumptuous female bestiality but on a
page of magical Evocation. Startled though I was,
my bowels had a great determination to refrain from
being sick.

I hurried to finish my toilet appointment (I had to
work from the memory of a camel I once knew) then
rushed to my study to progress my visions of the
magical text further.

I was truly astonished, and truly ashamed; upon
reading the script I found I had subconsciously
stuck a tomato on the end of my cock.

This knowledge now do I write-down for you. I have
seen them, all of them. I have been thrown before
the throne of Heme and I have been fondled within
the Plane Of Pain. All shall I explain to you later
but for now you must choose your path of light or of
darkness. I chose darkness and thus did I progress
my studies. However, my discoveries threaten
mankind and, as a last hope of salvation I write
down all that I know so that you may still fight

this evil.

And that my arse may be spared the red-hot poker in Hell.

Ah! May the Almighty save my arse from such prodding's, I implore thee have mercy!

As it is written:

To know your enemy is to overcome a large part of uncertainty.

Only by knowing your inner-level of viscous, cross-referenced with prior knowledge of the splash factor can you correctly fathom how many sheets to use during wipage. A mistake either way could prove costly, in terms of decency or sheets.

Thus by knowing your enemy can you overcome him [it].

Some may attempt to use the powers herein for personal gain or for cursing purposes. I tell you it cannot be done. Keep a clear head at all times and remember your goals. Summoning the Roids is not bad; knowledge of your enemy is needed. However, linger within the forces of The Greatest Red and you become entangled within The Everlasting Stance, of which there is no escape and no hope.

As assistance to your path I here provide a history of all, and a premise of what is to be, as written within my Orders papers.

And remember always: Beware the Monkey, for he is neither Man nor Woman nor Nun, but a Hairy Bastard.

The Beginning Of The Universe

In the beginning there was a pub.

The pub was of mock-Tudor styling and was a Free House, since at the beginning of the universe the concept of the 'Brewery' had not yet gained conception.

And the pub was called The Railway.

There was a particular client of the Free House who liked a bit of a drink. His name was Gordon, though everyone knew him as Gord.

Now Gord didn't work as such, since there are only so many openings of employment within a universe that consists solely of a Free House pub. He was unemployed. However, thought belies conception and so Gord was never short of money or pork scratchings.

For a living-of-sorts Gord painted portraits of people. His business wasn't going too well due to his artistic characteristics; he didn't have any. Also, he was quite, quite drunk for most of The (note that time had not yet been conceived, so the ending of the sentence with 'The', referring to everything, is quite correct).

One day Gord, wanting to try a different drink (other than Scrumpy) ordered a dark-looking liquid from the bar. Staring into the dark liquid for some time he waited whilst it settled, then gulped a mouthful.

Gee Whiz, pronounced Gord. However, under his foamy muffle all that could be heard was Gne Nniz.

As Gord sat back down behind his table at his
window seat, he peered out. All was nothing.

Drinking again from his pint glass he felt a
little odd. Growls cried up from his belly as a
reminder that he'd once pledged himself to Scrumpy
(and Pork Scratchings). Another growl and Gord
was sick.

Most of the sacred sick spattered down Gords-top in
a most unholy fashion, sinking into the very fibres
of his Pringle jumper. Some ran down his jumper,
fuelled with too much velocity to adhere to the
fibrous grip of the Pringle and splattered upon the
flagstone floor, to be licked-up by a three-legged
dog (who was also blind in one eye).

Of the least majority of the sick, some splattered
into his pint glass, sinking down and hanging there,
suspended within the thick, black liquid.

And thus the Universe was born of Physical.

Gord, having just been sick went to sleep,
slightly disappointed as he'd not yet told people
about his imaginary Lover; Munky. Thus the great
Period of Sleeping was entered.

And thus the Universe, charged with the dreams of
Gord was given life.

And as the creamy head upon the pint of Black
succumbed to chemical reaction and thus reverted
into the Blackness below, so too does our
Universe expand.

We await the great Period of Waking, where it is
fabled that Gord will awake freely from his slumber
and, as a consequence of the great Period of

Yawning, our Universe will experience the Great Tipple, upon which it is our destiny to either seep through the pub flagstone-cracks or be lapped-up by the three-legged dog (blind in one eye; huge pair of bollocks).

But fear not as this isn't the end for mankind. For we will be Reincarnated during the great Period Of The Vod, whereupon our Universe shall once again be rekindled within a bottle of Smirnoth Ice.

Our real fear should reside in a pre-universe fable, which dictates that when the man frozen in ice is awoken from his slumber, all shall cease to be. It is fabled that the only items keeping the man alive are his intoxication with alcohol (which, on balance of volume has stopped his blood from freezing), the fact that his king size kebab with chilli sauce is acting like a sort-of biological sleeping bag, and his dreams. The man froze whilst enraptured within a fascinating dream of endless blackness, within which there stood a pub, a Free House of mock-Tudor design.

This may never happen; the man may never awake. If, through a process of time the kebab ingests the man, then he shall never wake. His consciousness and thus his dreams will be digested by the kebab and thus all, everything, The, will be sustained within the consciousness of a [man-eating] kebab. Which may be preferable to all and everything being sustained within the consciousness of a human.

Joseph has listed two theories about whom this 'man' may be. His first theory lists that the man may be an ancient Tibetan Monk who, upon an ancient pilgrimage to Holy things at the top of a mountain got caught short by bad weather. As the Holy Man fought for survival he desperately pulled out his kebab (made of Monkey-flaps), knowing full well that on the one side it was his only means of survival but, on the otherside knowing full well that it may one day ingest him. He froze before he could find out. Joseph states that the level of alcohol present in the Monk was usual. "They're all at it", as he so succinctly puts it. As to why he froze so quickly and so completely, apparently the Monk came across a Mountain Monkey, who flashed him. The Monk, by order of natures law got his cock out and tried to chase the Mountain Monkey, who'd already skipped-off up a tree somewhere.

Joseph's second theory is that a man had been out drinking in Manchester. On his way home he purchased a kebab from one of the many excellent kebab restaurants in Manchester and made his way to the train station. Whilst behind Victoria Station having a piss, the man was propositioned by a hairy prostitute. The man, by order of nature dropped his trousers but was caught short by the vicious Manchester Wind. The man was already in the process of eating the kebab but this did him no good. Against the Wind the meagre hair of his scrotum afforded no protection. The prostitute, though chilled to her dirty bones escaped with her life. Were it not for her long hair, brillo-pad moustache, and Glen-Hoddle-Hair beard, she too would have perished. Joseph still thinks that the man is frozen in an alley near Victoria Station, lying erect behind a Wheelie Bin. Slowly the kebab ingests him, which in a way is ironic, since it was he whom had wished to digest the juicy kebab.

The reading of this parable seems to have changed Joseph somewhat. He quotes on the page "I will always seek to serve the Kebab to the best of my abilities. Even if it belongs to a right dog".

The Origin Of The Roids

The first creature to populate our universe was the Badger. Millions of years later the Badger would have it's entire civilisation turned upside down and would be forced underground due to the 'copyist' Horses, Skunks and Zebra Crossings whom stole the Badgers 'Look'.

However there was another creature, another being spawned from the hand [mind] of Gord: Munky. During roughly the same period Adam was conceived, purely by accident. Gord tried to imagine Munky naked and as thought belies conception so Adam was created from nought; the naked Munky.

Munky, who was not strictly speaking of a female gender (it was just hairy), was so upset by this whole affair that it pleaded with Gord to allow it wings, so that it may fly from this beastly planet and explore the Universe. Gord, still in love with his imaginary lover granted this wish and thus Munky became a winged beast. However, so that the beast would never forget Gord and leave him for another deity, Gord adorned Munky's loins with fire.

And so Munky flew away from Earth on a fruitless expedition. And it spent many years away, as a goldfish within a very large bowl until it returned.

Munky had been away a long time and upon its return, it had picked up a new skill; it could lay eggs.

Munky selected a remote field and laid its eggs, intent on spawning a race of its own.

Adam, now a grown man able to drink beer exited the only pub on Earth. Gord had erected a pub from memory, so there were some oddities. The pub itself was under a vast lake of alcohol into which people (Adam) dived, sat on a stool and simply opened his mouth for refreshment. Gord had also created a busty barmaid for Adam called Denise (Eve for short). She swam up and down the bar, bubbly personality mixed with a massive pair of baps; always wet.

So Adam, intoxicated from his drinking at the underwater bar decided to make his way home.

On his way home he entered a field for the sole intention of relieving himself. He stood there, under the full moon having a pee. When finished Adam tried to put his penis away but, trousers round-ankles he fell bottom-first upon Munky's eggs. The eggs were fatally ingested by Adams anus.

Munky, at this point perched up a tree having Oral encounters with a banana, looked down in horror at his eggs.

"I curse you Adam," it shouted as it jumped out of the tree and pinned him to the ground. Munky's anger was clear. It pulled out its bright red cock and started to rape Adam, with the words:

"I curse you … um… Adam.
Fath-er of … argh… mankind and destroyer of …whoa… eggs. To you and your sooooooooooons May … ouch… you feel my redness And my FFFFIIIIIIRRRRRRREEEEEE Forrrrrr …uch… all of …awwww… timmmmme …Arggghhh You Fooking Bastard you…"

With that Munky departed Earth and left Adam, half-unconscious with a throbbing hole.

And thus the Roids were spawned.

Munky made true on its curse. Planted within Adam lay the seed of fire, a seed which would lay dormant for thousands of years, a seed which was planted to exterminate mankind in the most horrible way, a seed which spawned Heme, and with him his minions; the Roids.

Adam, once awake took some weeks to recollect his incident with Munky. In a revenge arse-on attack, Adam ambushed Dingo, the king Baboon. Adam cursed his race with a red-arse affliction to last as long as their species. And to this day Adams handy-work can be seen. In Zoos, photographs and Jungles. The Baboon. The keeper of the pant-siren.

It must be noted at this point that Gord was not happy with Munky. Munky used to be Gords imaginary lover but, after the accidental conception of naked Munky (Adam), Gord had granted Munky wings (due to Munkys displeasure). Munky had flown throughout the universe and became an ether-travelling Whore. Munky was anyone's for the price of a banana. The final straw came when Munky raped naked Munky (Adam) on Earth. Gord had had enough and imprisoned Munky within a tiny used bottle of miniature Whiskey. He banished Munky in the bottle to the depths of our universe, where it was to remain forever; to be eternally scorched by its own fiery loins.

The Monkey race of Earth have their own prophecy concerning Munky. For millions of years they had collected a percentage of bananas consumed and were constructing one enormous banana. However, a

third-of-the-way through, the banana was consumed
by a rather large Orang-utan. The monkey Elders
lay a curse upon the Orang-utan, called Raymond
Small, that for evermore himself and his kin shall
be of ginger persuasion. A grim fate indeed.
Raymond had eaten so much banana due to his
enormous greed, that his entire body mass imploded
and created Africa. Raymond's spirit was forever
banished to the Plane of Stench (previously the
Plane of Little Kittens) within the Kingdom of
Heme.

The Monkeys, under instruction from the Elders now
started a new strategy. Rather than take a
percentage of bananas, all bananas were used. The
idea of the Elder Monkey's was to build such a large
banana that its smell would reach Munky, wherever it
may be lying in the stars. Motivated by the smell of
this gigantic banana, Munky would breakout of its
miniature Whiskey bottle and travel back to Earth.
Once back on Earth Munky would unite the Monkey-
Kingdom and war would once again be declared on man.

The sexuality of Munky has oft been questioned.
Though Gord created Munky as an imaginary lover, we
cannot be certain that Munky was a female.
Recorded history states that Munky raped Adam, and
to accomplish that mammoth task Munky would have
needed a Phallus. However, it is also recorded in
history that Munky laid eggs. There is no mention
of Munky possessing Ladies bits, and also no
mention of how it was impregnated. The most-
logical theory extended from my priestly order is
that Monkey was asexual. Able to reproduce by
itself, not quite man, not quite women, not as far
gone as a tranny. Like a flower. With a cock.

As to Munkys action of rape upon Adam, it would
seem that this was a revenge attack for the anal

ingestion of its eggs. Therefore whether Munky was attracted to the same-sex, albeit of a difference race cannot really be answered. Also, Adam was created as a naked Munky, and Adam was a man. Logically then it follows that Munky is also Male. But with the ability to lay eggs.

Unless the above prophecy comes true then surely we shall never really know. After all, Gord was very drunk when he created the universe and so anything is possible.

Of The First Coming

There have been two recorded Comings of Heme, and a third has been prophesied. This is a record of the First coming of Heme.

During the time of the dinosaurs was the period when Heme first surfaced amongst us. The dinosaurs started off as a simple evolution of Gords dream but soon they became independent consciousness-bubbles, totally defunct of Gords control.

Subsequently, the dinosaurs fell into an existence of debauchery and sexual deviance. These were just the ingredients needed to power the Coming of Heme and his fiery Roids.

The Roids came at first, subtle and 'magical' to observers: many thinking it was a new type of berry. At first they offered little more than slight discomfort, but that soon changed. Soon the Roids were able to control the very hosts which had fostered them.

And this epidemic was not limited to humans. The dinosaurs had been spawned of the same imagination that had firstly spawned Adam, and so they too inherited Adams Munky-curse.

The monkeys too were not safe. Brief and often unsatisfying nighttime encounters with drunken primitive man had passed-on Adams curse to the very species which had initiated the Roid.

All were afflicted with the red-berry of fire. The larger the hindquarters of the host, the worse the problem was and thus the greater number of Roids grew.

The Roids soon became a disability to their host, denying a sit-down and, in the extreme cases denying any movement at all.

At the peak of the outbreak, when almost every living creature on Earth was infected, Heme rode forth upon his Hairy Green Turtle.

Thus the Earth was plunged into the Aeon of the Long Stand. It was impossible for affected persons to be seated, and almost impossible for them to manoeuvre during hunting. Thus the creatures of Earth started to die both of starvation, exhaustion and embarrassment.

Gord did see his creatures dying and cast down a sacred balm to his creations so that they may combat the Roids. At this point both Munky and Heme had become independent conscious-bubbles (controlled by deep subconscious impulses) within Gords dreaming. Gord had no control of these two very real conjurations, just as the dinosaurs had escaped into independence.

Gord sent down his recipe for the Sacred Balm unto Earth. He cast it upon two stone tablets within the presence of the virgin Burning Bush (a local village girl. She was a Ginger, and hence a virgin to the fully sighted men in her village).

These tablets remained upon a small hill accessible to all. Dinosaurs, Monkeys and Humans travelled from all around to view the sacred ingredients upon the sacred tablets.

Unfortunately the dinosaurs had no arms with which to apply the Sacred Balm and so, unable to sit down or hunt, they were wiped out.

However, Humans and Monkeys succeeded in applying the Sacred Balm and so survived.

Then one cold, winters night a group of Humans stole the sacred tablets. And thus was born the everlasting Monkey War.

The war was bloody and brief, but quite easy. Because Monkeys couldn't write they had no record of the sacred ingredients of the sacred Balm. For the first hundred years the Monkeys fought. The Monkey-Elders retained the Balm-knowledge within their little furry heads. However, as the ingredients got passed-down Monkey generations through song, dance and shaped banana-pies, it became muddled. The Monkeys knew something had gone wrong when the ingredients included a Duracell battery as taken from the arse of a virgin marathon-running plastic rabbit.

It is written that he who holds the secret of the Sacred Balm has power over all living things whom may haveth a bunghole.

And so the Monkeys conceded and the war was over.

Monkeys were banished as a subservient species to man and, as per the terms of the agreement were never to develop any languages, power tools, fuel-efficient combustion engines or fast-food chains. On these conditions, the Humans promised that if Heme should ever again raise his ugly red head that the Balm would be given, once again, to the Monkeys.

At this point a secret Human society, known as The Keepers Of Cream, or KOC, dictated to society that the letter 'R' should be removed from the alphabet to keep Heme and his Roids at bay. For without the word Roid in their language the Roids could not take any form (to conceive is to form). This decision had five main consequences upon Human evolution:

1) The name of the Great Creator Gord, was now deemed to be against the best interests of Human society and so it was changed to God. There were still those who persistently referred to The Creator as Gord, though these people were generally hung up by their testicles.

2) Women were banned from speaking, since they had difficulties in omitting 'R' from their tongue. During lovemaking primitive woman had to be gagged. Some women thought out about this, thinking out loud that the practice was 'barbaric' and should be outlawed. Other women thought out that it was just a bit of fun, and always went to bed with a twinkle in their eye. The knock-on effect of this was that women would also, as per the Monkeys, take a subservient role for millions of years to come.

3) All peoples of the name 'Rupert' were considered so far gone down the 'R' route that they were unable to change their names. Under the new terms and conditions for Human society they were executed. By coincidence this was about the time that large rocks became the norm for dashing ones brains about the place; thus Stoning was born. The effect of this new law was that many Rupert's were driven underground and became part of a terrorist movement, led by Rupert the Bare (so called because of his absence of a loin cloth and his passion for travelling everywhere on stilts). It was rumoured that the Amend Rupert Stoning's for Ever (or A.R.S.E)

communed with the Monkeys, hence members of
A.R.S.E tended to become extra hairy.
Rupert the Bare left A.R.S.E after a while
as it was becoming too soft: he had always
advocated that members in A.R.S.E should be
forever rock-hard. He started an off shoot
of A.R.S.E called, originally, The Order of
the Roid: their symbol being the venomous
crack-fruit. The Order, unlike A.R.S.E,
permitted all peoples to join: even those
people whose name didn't even contain an
'R'. However, he did not remain as OHO of
this organisation long... Rupert the Bare
fell from grace quite literally when, upon
treading on a discarded banana peel he came
crashing to the ground, stilts and all.
His loin cloth detached from his bulk and
his members observed a smooth moon with a
cream of Ral-Lief soaked Valley. And
within his cleft, held tightly by a
practised straining, sat a business card
containing an emergency phone number for
the Keepers Of Cream. It would appear that
Rupert could no longer take the pain
demanded by his master Heme and so had
changed sides. Rupert was booted out but
the Order continued unto this day, with
many members not of the name Rupert. Many
cults roam the lands as a Carnival of Anal
Anguish.

4) The lack of an adequate replacement for the
letter 'R' within primitive mans alphabet
meant that they reverted to cave paintings
(using non-inflammatory colours, i.e. those
that did not contain 'R' in their name;
thus the tradition of giving colours silly
names began). This, whilst being the only
solution at the time also effected a two

thousand year reversal of mans civilised-
development. The Keepers of the Cream
became zealots. They had representatives
in each and every Human society to weed-out
the blasphemers and the Monkey-lovers.
People found practising the art of evoking
Heme (largely a spiteful practice carried-
out by members of A.R.S.E) had their anus'
sealed with what in modern terms could only
be called a metal baby's nappy with one-way
locking device and non-malleable butt plug.
Or a kinky sex toy.

5) With the absence of 'R' from the human
language people became rubbish at giving
directions (a trait which has stayed with
mankind to this day). There is a legend of
an ancient man, Breck Fast who once asked
directions in the ancient village of
Taunton. Breck, upon following directions
from a local prostitute, spent seven years
, seven days and seven minutes searching
for the post office. Only after his seven
years, seven days and seven minutes
searching did someone point out to him that
he'd been searching in a left-orientated
circle, which is why he came back to the
same spot at the start of each day. Breck,
upon hearing this news sat down in despair;
not only was the post office just off to
his right, but they wouldn't accept his
stamps as legal tender either. To top it
all the invitation he was sending for his
hosted dinner party was seven years out of
date. Upset by these facts Breck killed
himself. The great man Breck was turned
into a minor deity; one which we still
celebrate today with Breakfast. Like Breck
Fast, Breakfast starts each day in exactly

the same place.

The repercussions as detailed above were not met by disapproval from all however. The socialites of the day thought the proceedings far from grim. The 'Old School' were able to drag their cobweb-covered clubs out of their cupboards and start 'clubbing' again. And thus the term 'clubbing' was truly born. Its definition: A group of people placed together with alcohol, dark lights to cover the Uglies and loud music to cover any deficiencies in conversation, with the intentions of jiggling about a bit then having sex with no recollection of the other-party come the morning after.

Joseph comments; "Bastard Monkeys. I knew it. I went to Bristol Zoo and one of the bastards pinched my ice cream. I chased it into a corner and smashed its head-in with the bottom of my boot. It was a real mess; I fed the bits to the Lions. I got my ice cream back. Strawberry flavour yum. Bastard flake had been eaten though." He also adds "It was fabled that over-application of the Sacred Balm, as carried-out by the most-zealot members of the Keepers Of Cream, could prolong life albeit with the side-affect of turning your hair grey and turning you into a bit of a nonce. Through my research and psychic visions I think that Peter Stringfellow is the last remaining 'Old School' Clubber/Zealot. Notice how the girls that are with him never speak… Next time you see Peter Stringfellow, ask him what's in his purse. Full of gags I'll bet (not the funny kind, the not-able-to-say-R type).."

Of The Second Coming

The Second Coming of Heme was thwarted.

By the time of Heme's Second Coming (approx 0 BC/AD by the Christian calendar) the Earth had changed a lot.

People had grown and forgotten about the teachings of their ancestors. Thus their knowledge of Heme and his Roids was forgotten. The Keepers Of Cream had long-since retired into a most-secret organisation known to none but yet feared by all.

Society too had changed. Social orgies and deviance provided once again fuel for the Roids fire. By far the most influential change to society however, had been the re-introduction of the letter 'R'.

The reintroduction of the letter 'R' came about by two main factors:

1)   Members in A.R.S.E had infiltrated into top government positions. From these positions they were able to pursue legislation to reinstate the letter 'R', and to once again make 'Rupert' a non-punishable-by-death name.

2)   Politicians had succumbed to public demand. People wanted to use the word 'Roger' as a humorous representation of the action of jumping inside a person and having a bit of a jiggle.

Thus did the letter 'R' make 'Roid' a true word again, and by action of thought gave Heme power. And thus did he awaken.

Heme came forth before his minions did this time.
He intended to be there from the start, to direct
operations. However, Heme arriving first meant
that he didn't have the usual protection afforded
to him by his countless minions. He decided to
brave it and to start proceedings alone.
Ultimately this proved to be his downfall.

Heme rode forth into Nazareth upon the
hindquarters of a donkey (upon the ass of an ass).

All was going well until, the Ass left unattended,
it was beset by some playful children. The playful
children decided to kick the ass in the ass and
thus Heme, in his physical manifestation was pulped
into a squidgy mess.

His body broken and his juices scattered, Heme
retreated back to his palace. His second assault
had proven much less effective than his first; he'd
have to ponder a further strategy, one infinitely
more sinister…

Joseph made little comment here, marking his
parchment with a single tear. And some tomato seeds
(at this point I think Joseph's affection for the
lusty fruit was starting to take effect). He also
noted "Heme's will to come first during his second
coming proved his downfall. Some think Heme was
being selfish; I think pragmatic. Sometimes it is
better to come second; sometimes it is unavoidable
to come second. Bare this in mind. Learn to come
second, or come together with your people. Everyone
coming in harmony (to the sound of a drum beat if
you have one). I'd like to teach the Roids to come.
In perfect harmony".

Of The Third Coming

The Third Coming of Heme has yet to take place but be warned, this will be the most cunning attack by the Roids yet.

Although his second coming upon the ass of an ass was thwarted by children kicking the ass in the ass, Heme will come again (it is prophesied) upon the arse of a Monkey.

The place of his coming is prophesied to be the holiest of all holy places, the city of eternal light, the city of a thousand-thousand pilgrimages; the city with the greatest football team, prettiest women and tastiest kebabs in the world. The City of Manchester.

It is written thus :

Heme will ride forth upon the arse of a Monkey into the Holy City of Manchester. No one will kick the Monkey in the arse, as he shall be of black and white, of short stature and with tiny grasping hands. He shall be a spider monkey, dressed as a miniature hairy clown with big shoes and a plastic flower that shoots water with a burst of humour. Nay, this time Heme shall not be stomped. And every person who touches the Monkey in its special place shall become a vessel for Heme's Roids. And the Monkey will jump on people, rubbing their chins with its excrement soaked fur and thus creating lesser Roids upon the host. This is to be carried out in agreement with the Monkey King, for when Heme rules over mankind he has promised to help the monkeys with the construction of their gigantic banana.

Preceding this event, or at around the same time there will be a second war between man and monkey.

Man will have erected huge prison-fortresses called Monkey Prisons, into which all monkey POWs and criminals will be flung with no right of appeal or to an attorney.

Within the Monkey Prison life will be hard. Inmates will be wheeled from section to section for fear that they will attempt to leap out of the compound, even though their legs shall be chained and the prison will be encased within a dome of wire mesh. Still, it'll be for their own good. Less walking to do. Ungrateful hairy feckers.

It is prophesied that through Human greed the monkeys will win this second war. It is said that a large Western power will train the monkeys to fight in third world countries that are really nothing to do with it, save the interest of its corporations.

These monkeys will abscond and take the training and the weapons back to the forest, where King Monkey will instigate combat training and technical awareness for all his monkey-minions.

Thus it shall be that the hand of man and the greed in his belly will overthrow world order, and make way for the rule of the monkey.

After this, when humans shall be packed into the once Monkey Prisons and taken out only to work on the monkey banana plantations, Heme shall turn his attention to the monkeys.

With no ability to write things down, and with the power of the KOC all but destroyed there shall be no remedy for this anal assault. The monkeys too shall become enslaved.

All will be decided at the great battle: when Munky

is released from the miniature Whiskey bottle to return to Earth and free his people from anal tyranny. On this date will Munky and Heme do battle. And the fate is undecided since both Heme and Munky are subconscious entities and so are not controlled by the dreamings of Gord.

Joseph adds :

"Evidence of the once-plentiful Cults of the Roid can be found today in the numerous Standing Stone Circles of Earth. The Circle of Stone; Natures ring piece.

Also said to be built upon Ley Lines; sacred lines of power. Thus the Circles are constructed upon magical cracks; the buttock-clefts of the Earth (for there are many).

Bogs were also considered as entry points into Mother Earths arsehole; hence history is scattered with numerous so called 'Bog Burials'.

So it can be seen that primitive man thought the Kingdom of Heme to be resident within the arsehole of Mother Earth. His thoughts can now be proven to be incorrect: Mother Earth doesn't have a literal arsehole.

She simply harvests those that are".

Of The Snake

The Snake is a re-occurring symbol with the Roid Mythos.

It can be fathomed that the snake should not be taken literally, as snakes are not afflicted with the condition of the Roid.

You must beware the snake, for it is an ally of the Roids and their evil intentions.

It is written that the snake was actually a worm living within Adams intestine along with its friends.

However, this worm was a bully and a pig, and used to steal the food of its fellow worms. Because of this it grew to a truly huge size.

Time took its course and happened upon expulsion of the worm. The worm didn't want to leave, but it had gotten stuck in Adams colon and so expulsion was inevitable.

After several weeks of pushing on the toilet, the worm was finally anally expelled by Adam.

Thus was born the Snake.

Upon birth the snake reared up and spoke to Adam:

Why did you expel me from your innards? I was having a lovely time. Well, Adam, creation of Gord the most-Holy, I hereby pledge allegiance of all snake folk, of which I am the first, and all worm folk, of which I used to be, to the Roids. We will serve them, and carry them forth upon our tides of expulsion. You know, we could have been friends you and me. We're not all that different, you and I. We both dream, we both eat, we both enjoy cricket. But now you've blown it, all because I'm a snake. What's the matter, snakes not good enough to live within your anal passage? Well I don't care. I'll find my own food. I've heard that apples are quite nice. Yessssss, apples! I'll grow myself an apple tree with fruit as red as a Roid. Goodbye Adam. May our paths never again cross.

With that the snake slithered away, muttering under its breath.

Adam did meet the snake again afterwards whilst picnicking with Eve amongst an Orchard. It turns out that the snake had a thriving cider business, but that's another story…

Joseph comments here

"The Snake was addicted to apples as, since the underwater pub was constructed by Gords memory, the only drink on offer was cider. Thus the only food eaten by the snake was indeed the humble apple".

Of The Monkey

The monkey is important within the Roid Mythos.
The monkey was spawned from the same matter as
man, though a bit more hairy. Although under terms
of the Monkey War agreement they haven't been able
to even start fast food chains (though they are
the industries staple workforce), they do live
within a structured society. Most species of
Monkey fit into mid-society, that is the monkey IT
workers, plumbers, lawyers etc. However, there
are certain species attributed with certain tasks.
They are detailed here, with the first species
being listed as the most-menial placement within
monkey society.

1) Orang-Utan. These beasts have, because of
   Raymond and his greed been given the worst
   placements within society. They are Ginger
   (which isn't strictly speaking work, though
   being Ginger is an occupation). Due to the
   curse of the monkey elders, Orang-Utans
   don't even loose their sickening-sheen
   during old age.

2) Spider Monkey. These monkeys form the
   core of monkey society. Spider Monkeys
   are the entertainers, the clowns; the
   prostitutes. Though being a prozzie
   may not be glamorous, within monkey
   society being a whore is much more
   preferable than being a ginge.

3) Howler Monkeys. These are the porn stars
   of the monkey world. The entire jungle
   comes-alive with the pleasurable yelps of
   Howler monkey love, and these monkeys have
   a lot of loving in them.

4) Chimpanzees are the monkey leaders. Due to
   their intelligence they can often be found

as political and religious leaders. Most
monkeys look up to the chimp as a great
source of direction and leadership.

5) Gorillas form the basis of the Monkey
   Unified Fighting Forces, or MUFF.
   Gorillas, due to their size make incredible
   warriors. Often they are lead by a chimp
   mounted on a larger gorilla. Due to the
   size of the gorilla, they are most
   venerable to Roid anal attack.

6) Baboons, the keepers of the pant siren are
   monkey shamans. As well as possessing vast
   occult knowledge of herbs and magic
   dealings, the baboons have the disturbing
   ability to talk to coconuts. Senior
   Baboons can also cause their arses to flash
   a physcodelic pattern of Red. This could
   prove useful in high seas, as a distress
   beacon. This skill has never yet been used
   in anger. It's also useful for lighting a
   Monkey Disco. Most baboons venture onwards
   to become Monkey Elders.

All other monkey species fit within the middle-
society, as detailed previously.

The monkey society is ruled over by the Monkey
King. The Monkey King rotates through the species
on a fixed rotary basis, though an Orang-Utan can
never be King. The Monkey King once survived a
coupe, as initiated by a large Western power that
abandoned the rebels once the coupe failed. The
Monkey King slaughtered the rebels and bought
weapons from the same Western power, weapons used
to oppress his peoples for years after.

Due to this experience, the Monkey King maintains
and pays for MUFF. The MUFF is organised thus:

- 100 Monkeys = Monkey Warband

- 1000 Monkeys = Monkey Army

- 10000 Monkeys = Monkey Division

- 100000 Monkeys = Monkey Legion

Due to the emergence of the Internet the King's MUFF has been able to acquire knowledge required for fighting a modern war. They have also been able to train themselves within their secret monkey training camps, perfecting their guerrilla tactics for the forthcoming conflict.

As well as liking MUFF, the Monkey King also likes to enforce two other activities:

1) Monkeys have to become 'Banana Gatherers' for a period of their lives. This is decided by a rotary system going back to the extinction of the dinosaurs. Their job is to gather bananas for the construction of the Giant Banana and thus the return of Munky. When seen in public it may look like the monkeys are actually eating the banana. You'd be wrong. The monkey is actually tapping-off the banana down a plastic tube and into a plastic bag they have concealed upon their person via hairy netting. Like a piss bag, only for Monkeys not old people or pop stars. All this pulp is then sent back to the Monkey Kingdom for inclusion within the Giant Banana.

2) The Monkey King personally overseas the running of the Monkey PR department. The department frequents zoos and foreign governments, preaching the values of Monkeeism within an ever-more disenchanted world. They also amuse human children, planting the seed into their minds that monkeys are cute, monkeys are mans friends.

Of The Banana

The Banana was conceived before Hemes First Coming but, because the banana is of female gender, decided not to develop its own speech due to the very real chance of being persecuted. And so the banana sat speechless and, even today the banana does not chat. Because of this, and because of its short life expectancy the banana also felt it unnecessary to develop limbs of any sorts. And because it didn't talk, the banana thought it wise to dispense with eyes, for any external temptation was not wanted. Thus the banana developed into just a head; its brain encased within a protective skin.

Because of the bananas fears it thus developed into a brain, and as the only thing a brain does is think, so the banana became super intelligent. Some would argue that it didn't become intelligent enough to sprout limbs; fair enough, though if this was Gords intention then it would have so been. If any race became aware of this fact and managed to harvest the computing power of the banana, then that race would surely exceed its brothers and sisters.

Due to the bananas lack of speech, it is implicitly safe for a monkey to make love to a banana. Hence the phrase "Monkeys love bananas" should be taken as a literal term.

He who seeketh the Red Berry shall find them, and within them shall be revealed the Truth. -Joseph. 41

Of The Trinity: Three is the Magic Number

There is a symbol which encompasses the beginning of creation: The Trinity.

The Trinity actually used to be the Quadruple, but the Badgers didn't like the idea of their stripe being used as a logo and so they absconded in a huff. No Stripes, no Gripes.

The Trinity is a universal symbol that represents the first entities of creation (except the Badger). Hence the Trinity is drawn thus:

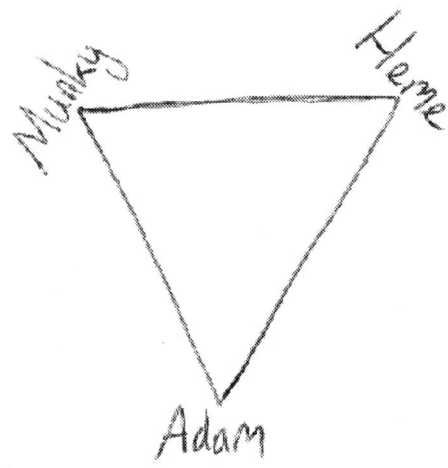

There is no Gord present on the Trinity, as Gord is everywhere.

Eve isn't explicitly shown on the symbol as she is represented implicitly by the inverted triangle: her throbbing Quim and thus her gift to all womenfolk (and some whole-hog trannies too: modern surgery is truly amazing in its power to butcher and deform).

As Eve giveth power with the Carpet of Eros, so too does she forsake dignity with periodic front-bottom diarrea. Like a thatched volcano erupting. Or a poorly Mussel.

The Trinty can be represented by a single word, made from reading Heme, Adam and Munky clockwise: HAM. This is the word of the Trinity.

LIBER 1 :: OF THE ROIDS

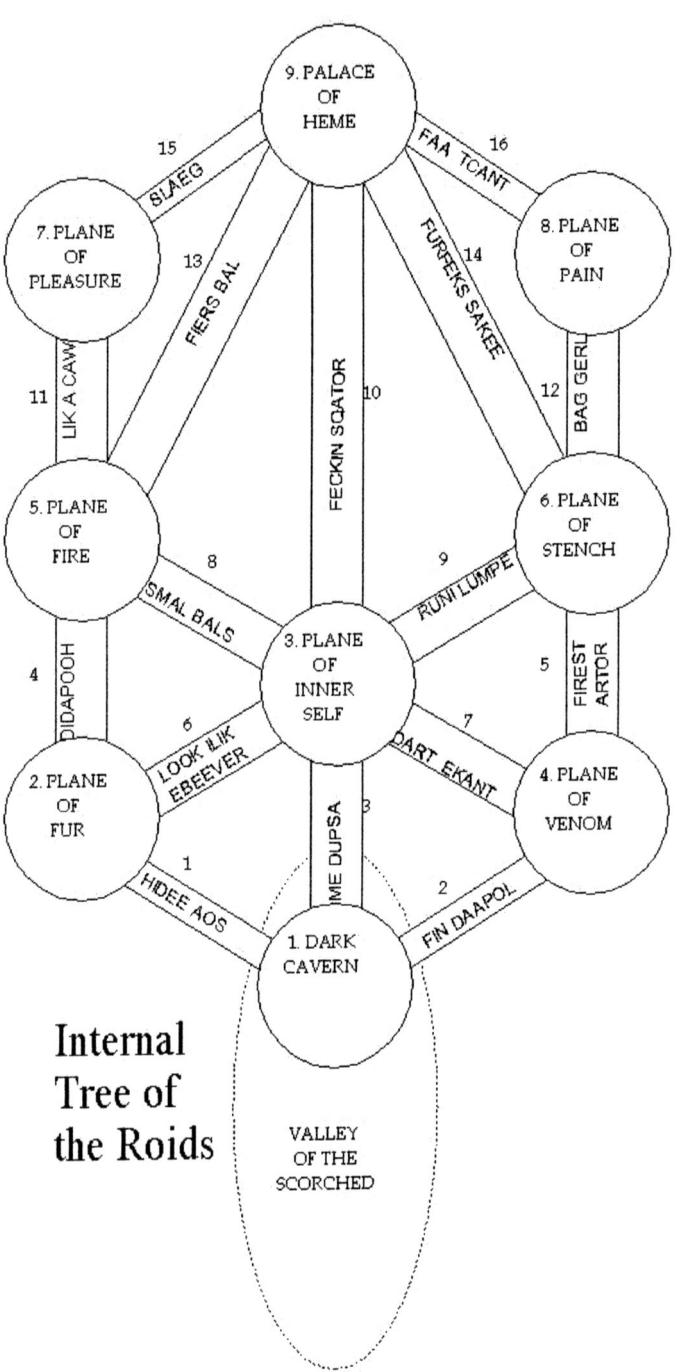

Internal Tree of the Roids

9. PALACE OF HEME

15 SLAEG
16 FAA TCANT

7. PLANE OF PLEASURE

8. PLANE OF PAIN

13 FIERS BAL
14 FURREKS SAKEE

11 LIK A CAW
12 BAG GERL

10 FECKIN SQATOR

5. PLANE OF FIRE

6. PLANE OF STENCH

8 SMAL BALS
9 RUNI LUMPE

3. PLANE OF INNER SELF

4 DIDAPOOH
5 FIREST ARTOR

6 LOOK LIK EBEEVER
7 DART EKANT

2. PLANE OF FUR

4. PLANE OF VENOM

1 HIDEE AOS
3 ME DUPSA
2 FIN DAAPOL

1. DARK CAVERN

VALLEY OF THE SCORCHED

Lore Of The Roids

The Roids are a daemon manifestation conceived by Munky not long after the start of the Universe.

Munky chose to curse mankind because Adam destroyed its eggs. Adam in fact was created by mistake as the image of a naked Munky, hence when Munky descended from the tree and raped Adam, he was in fact committing an action of deviant self-love.

However, the self-love was fuelled by anger and, during Munky's curse to Adam (made during the self-abuse), the fire of Munkys loins was transferred into his seed, which implanted itself firmly up Adams bum.

Fuelled by the curse and angry conception the seed turned into a kingdom, not contained physically within Adams arse but conceptually. No one's arse is large enough to contain a kingdom (Joseph notes: except maybe John Prescott), but rather the colon contains a link, an astral anchor to the kingdom of the Roids. By launching yourself into the astral, and by following certain rituals given herein you can be directed into, and indeed enter into the Kingdom. But be warned. The Roids are a protective community and you must be on your guard. The protection rituals also given herein are useful during any visits to the Kingdom but there is no substitution for protection by wit.

There have been tales of woe concerning scholars of the past who dared enter the Kingdom. Some of these scholars were taken prisoner or else seduced by SLAEG (the Roid temptress and harlot), never to return from their astral to their body. They had literally got their [astral] heads stuck up their arses.

Modern science has failed to understand the Roids
correctly. Thus they have been labelled as
'haemorrhoids' within modern society. This
conjunction of terms has come about due to ancient
knowledge being lost (or considered so silly as to
have no place within a modern world). I pity
these fools, for by their ignorance they not only
threaten themselves but threaten the ring of
mankind.

Here, within this book shall be presented the true
descriptions of the Roids along with their leader,
Heme. Take heed of these writings, especially so if
you wish to enter their kingdom. Remember that
knowledge is power, and without it you will be as a
rat within a maze, being chased by red Pac Man type
characters, all wanting a piece of your arse.

You have been warned.

"They preach that Light has power over Darkness, but
has it? Place a lighted candle in a darkened room
and the Blackness is repelled; revoked. But it is
inevitable that the candle shall burn dry. And then
what? All returns to Darkness; all returns to no
thing.

The Sun may rise in the sky and, for a moment of
hours there is light. But hear that! It rises to
give us light! Darkness neither rises nor sets.
Darkness is ambient. Darkness is everywhere.
Darkness is the Universes consequence." - Joseph.
41.

The Internal Tree Of The Roids

The 'Internal Tree of the Roids', sometimes called
the 'Infernal Internal Tree of the Roids',
represents an abstraction of the Kingdom including
Planes and Paths.

Ancient man knew of this tree and when the human
society sanctions took effect (when the letter 'R'
was removed from the alphabet) they abbreviated it.
They took the highlighted letters shown here
'**Int**ernal Tree **of the R**o**id**s', and added a **V** to
represent the 'Valley of the Scorched': the entry-
point into the Kingdom. This created the word 'Into
the Void', which ancient man used to refer to the
'map' of the kingdom. You may choose either name for
the 'map', as the letter 'R' has now been reinstated
as part of the human alphabet (without prosecution).

Whichever name you wish to use, each has its own
Sigil. This Sigil is to be used during the ritual
of 'Entering the Kingdom'. The Sigil helps your
subconscious to align your astral with the Kingdom's
astral anchor (within your psychic colon).

A Plane (or Disc) is a location within the Kingdom.
Know now that the Kingdom lives within you, though
astrally and as such Planes map onto specific parts
of your physical [body]. There are 9 such planes,
numbered 1-9 on the diagram. Each plane has
specific qualities and characteristics. It should be
remembered that the diagram is only an abstract
representation of the Kingdom, which itself is an
abstract concept of a representation of astral-
physical conception.

The diagram also has 16 paths, or 16 Tunnels Major.
The Kingdom comprises of many thousands of paths,
roads and tunnels. However, there are only 16
'true' paths that will take you directly between

Planes. Be wary of this, as you could get lost
within the lesser paths of the Kingdom: do not stray
from the Tunnels Major. Imagine them as motorways
within a Kingdom comprised of A and B roads. Avoid
these roads and stay on the Motorways.

Each Path has an associated Greater Roid. This
Greater Roid is a master daemon employed by Heme to
watch the Tunnels Major and stop any unwanted
travellers. Be wary of these daemons, for they are
powerful. However, each has weaknesses which can be
exploited by the wary (and knowledgeable) traveller.
Descriptions of the Greater daemons will be
presented later.

The appearance of Planes may differ from person to
person. However, they each have similar
characteristics which shall be explained below, as
well as their Sigils.

But first, a word on the Anal Snakes.

"And as darkness quickened me into a charmed
slumber, I looked down upon the black stream below
and saw nought therein but a false death". Joseph.
41.

The Anal Snakes

The Kingdom is populated with worms: Anal Snakes.

These Snakes are captured and trained at birth by the Roids to protect their Kingdom from intruders. That means you!

The Snakes appear as gelatinous elongated-tubes. They seem to float down the passages of the Kingdom but are really pushing themselves along on thousands of nearly invisible hairs.

If you see a Snake and are inexperienced at astral fighting then run. In any case, even if you are experienced it may be preferable to run. The Snakes will drain your energy and, if you are defeated they will literally suck you dry, sending you back to your shell on Earth with mental deteriation (such as a split personality). In the worst cases people have returned depressed by being ginger, when in fact they are not ginger. Snakes can be cruel.

Be on your guard at all times once inside the Kingdom, as the Snakes can sense intruders from a great distance.

However, the Snakes are simple creatures and will shy away from fire. The problem here is that it isn't always best to traverse the Kingdom with exposed flame. The Kingdom is full of potentially explosive gases.

Therefore, you will find on your travels through the Kingdom that an astral-budgie in an astral cage is essential. Should the budgie die, extinguish your flame immediately. High-powered torches are not as effective as fire for keeping the snakes at bay.

However, if you do decide to use an astral electrical torch on your travels make sure its batteries are fully charged. The Kingdom possesses no stockists of electrical goods.

As a last resort if confronted by a Snake, ask it sympathetically "What does a Snake do when it has an itch?". The Snake will most likely ponder this question then skulk away. If the Snake is not impressed by your riddler-wisdom then ask it "What is the noise of a single Snake clapping". Then run. That one won't keep them occupied for long...

As a final note on the Anal Snakes, they tend not to wear shoes. However, they have been observed traversing the Kingdom wearing a single, large slipper.

"The Egyptians built huge pyramids to honour their goddess: their Eve; Isis. With her back upon the golden sands she lies there [sunbathing], her legs stretching upwards towards the skies. Her toes caress constellations perched way up in the black-appetite of the universe. And as the seasons here on Earth change, so the constellations do drift and so too does the land change from barren to fertile and back again. The toes of Eve stay resting upon these constellations, and as she stretches towards the sky, legs akimbo, so too is the land made fertile. When the long legs of Eve come once again to closure, the land is barren and dull of growth. Thus the fertility of the land can be gauged by the spread of Eves legs. The pyramid serves as a mathematical anchor-point for Eve, for it represents her gift to womenfolk: the carpet of Eros as abstracted into stone. Only high priests were allowed into her abstracted gusset. Thus it can be said that Egypt invented the practise of the gynaecologist, in a way.

You see the Pyramids were never meant to be a place of death. They were meant to be a place of rebirth. This is why great Kings and Queens rested here: to be reborn and pumped out into the afterlife; to ascend.

The land of Egypt was robbed of its fertility when the Pyramids began to crumble. Famine and social decline followed. Egypt never did fully recover from Eve's menopause". Joseph. 41.

The Astral Baby

Much worse than the Anal Snakes is the Astral Baby.
The Baby wonders the paths of the Kingdom spouting
it's shrill wail-of-Death. Should you ever be
subjected to the wail-of-Death then the insides of
your head will melt; your brain will bleed.

Standing ten-feet high at a crawl and armed with a
rattle, giant rabbit soft toy and teething trouble,
the Baby is a fearsome creature. It is rumoured
that the Baby wanders the paths of the Kingdom
looking for its mother.

No one really knows how the Astral Baby came
into being. However there are some theories:

1)   Baby was created from the unnatural
        union of Heme and Munky. On seeing the
        fruits of their lust they were both
        horrified and thus cast poor Baby deep
        into the pathways of the lower-Kingdom
        (where it is said lost travellers
        degenerate and turn into rotting
        cannibals).

2)   Baby used to be an astral traveller who
        became trapped in the Kingdom. The
        traveller had a baby fetish and, after
        years of entrapment has degenerated
        into that which he craves. This could
        possibly be the result of too much time
        spent within the Plane of Inner Self.

3)   Baby was, as Adam, an accidental
        creation by Go(r)d.

Whatever the reason for Baby's being, it is rumoured
that he/she (sex has not yet been determined) is

indestructible. Heme himself has tried to rid the Kingdom of Baby: he and a score of Roids rode forth upon Anal Snakes (Heme on his Hairy Green Turtle) to seek out and destroy Baby. All the Roids were destroyed and, were it not for the agility of Heme's Hairy Green Turtle he himself may have been destroyed. Baby is the only entity which scares Heme.

Baby isn't evil as such. It just wants its mummy. If someone were to know the true name of Baby then its power could be harnessed: that person would become unstoppable.

Remember that when you reach the summit of the Holy Mountain you will be able to see all, for all shall lie below you. And as you look down upon those below you, so too do they look up at you. -Joseph . 41

Wormholes within the Kingdom

Before describing the Planes that make up the Kingdom, it is necessary to discuss briefly the subject of astral wormholes within the Kingdom.

Wormholes are a fact. Within the Kingdom they may appear as a tunnel which gets progressively darker, a mirror which doesn't reverse your reflection, a secret passageway hidden in the back of a wardrobe or anything else at all.

Wormholes, unless you know what you're doing are to be avoided. Remember, if you venture down a wormhole you must be able to return.

As with telepathy Anal Wormholes link together different persons psychic colons. As the [psychic] colon contains the Astral Kingdom, it thus follows that the Kingdom is riddled with such wormholes, or psychic links to [everybody on the Earth's] psychic colons. Wormholes thus allow you to shorten your journeys within the Kingdom. But do be wary that if you do use the wormholes you will be travelling through other people's colons, in the psychic-sense (similar to mind reading, but colon-navigating via the shared astral Plane that is the Kingdom).

Please be very careful on your exit from the Kingdom. You MUST exit via your own Scorched Valley. To exit from another persons Scorched Valley is a BIG mistake, as things usually get very messy indeed.

Also be aware that whilst in the presence of another's colon you are subject to that person's interpretation of their private passage. You may encounter entities here whilst traversing a wormhole that are just as dangerous as any Roid. Be warned.

If the Anal Wormholes can be proven then it stands that everybody on this Earth is connected to the 'generic' Kingdom; There is only one Kingdom and so reason states that all must share it, and to share it one must be able to access it (hence the Wormhole). In Plane terms, the Dark Cavern is probably your wormhole (personal passage) into the Kingdom. Beware though as the Dark Cavern, as per all the Planes of the Kingdom, contains a myriad of passages and tunnel-ways.

Thus it stands that as well as everybody being connected to the Kingdom by Anal Wormholes, we are all connected to each other via the wormholes. Thus it can justly be said that mankind is one great-big arsehole.

Joseph states within one of his notebooks that when connected, the Anal Wormholes look somewhat like Wales or, depending upon your angle of perception, Anthea Turner. This is his picture.

Alphabet of the Roids

The Roids inherited language from their host, Adam. Since Adam was an Englishman it follows that the alphabet of the Roid can be successfully approximated to that of the English. There are many things attributed to the Roids from Adams influence including bowler hats, tea, Tupperware and a passion for a Queen. Heme's penchant for buggery can perhaps be traced back to Eve's Germanic influence.

ALPHABET OF THE ROID, INCLUDING ENGLISH AND NUMBER ASSOCIATION.

A 2, B 9, C 14, D 21, E 3, F 15, G 2, H 1, I 19, J 15
K 13, L 22, M 4, N 7, O 24, P 7, Q 5, R 12, S 20, T 10
U 26, V 16, W 6, X 23, Y 11, Z 8

* = Repeat Characters
_ = Letter underlined is a Capital. Eg □ = a , 🔲 = A

Examples;

hello World   Heme.

To work out the numerical value of a word, add the total of the letters. Duplicate letters cancel each other out in pairs. For example, a single D = 2, two D = 0, three D = $(2 + 2 + 2) 2$. A Capital is always counted. For example, the sequence DD = 2.

Example

= 1+3+4+3   = 4+3+21+26+0+2
= 1+4   = 76
= 5

Numeracy of the Roid

The Roids have developed a basic operation of Math. Though at first appearing cumbersome, the system is very easy to use. The system of Math is contained upon the Counting Disc (CD).

The system centres around Globe Containers, or GC's. The GC's are concentric and consist of layers. The centre, or Prime GC is used for representing units. Each additional GC is used to represent another unit X 10. For example, the second GC represents tens, the third hundreds etc.

Each GC, except the first is divided into three sections, called Trinity Sections (TS). Each section can hold up to three Globes. The Globes dictate an amount, so a single Globe equals a single unit within the GC. For example, three Globes within the third GC would be 300.

Fractions are represented by a double-banded GC, where the inner band is thicker than the outer. Roid fractions are limited to tenths.

Of course the CD can have as many GCs as required, though it is very rare for a Roid to be able to use numbers higher than 1 million (6 GCs).

The system of numeracy used by the Roids has dictated certain financial conditions for the populace of the Kingdom. For example, a money withdrawal of any significance can take a couple of days to work out, and anything up to a week of standing in Bank queues. Naturally this means that the Roid in question must be prepared to take time off work, for the Banks within the Kingdom are very unethical and only open during short daylight hours. There is no banking available for those Kingdom inhabitants who actually work for a living.

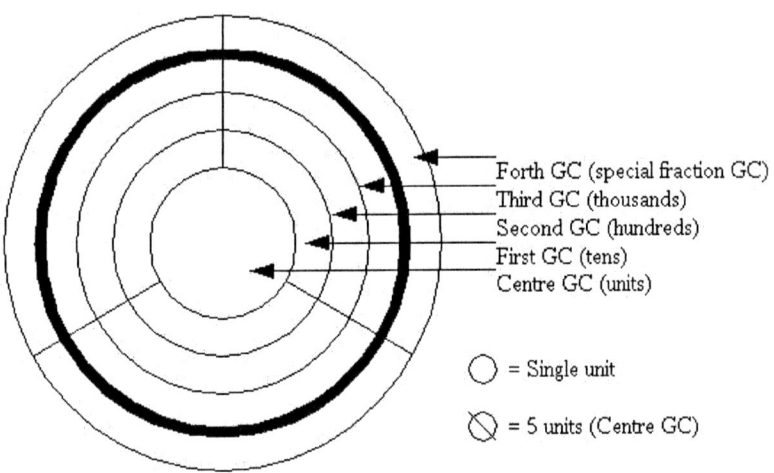

Forth GC (special fraction GC)
Third GC (thousands)
Second GC (hundreds)
First GC (tens)
Centre GC (units)

◯ = Single unit

⊘ = 5 units (Centre GC)

Example:

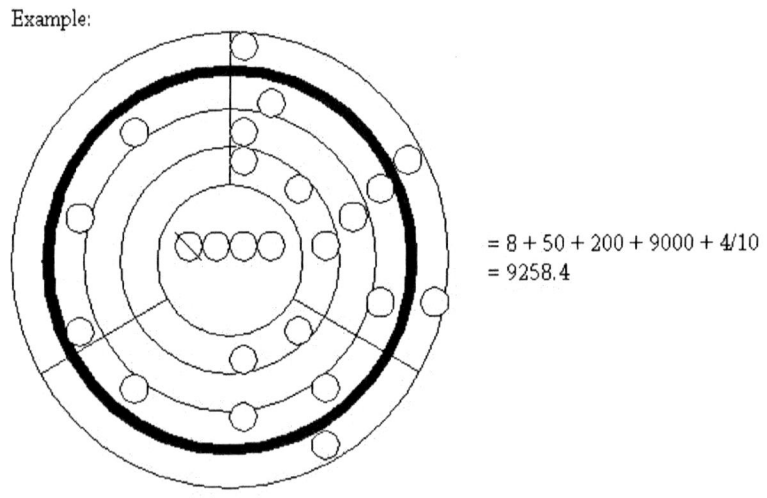

= 8 + 50 + 200 + 9000 + 4/10
= 9258.4

Valley of the Scorched

The Valley of the Scorched has no Sigil: it is the
entry into the Kingdom and can be found implicitly
by using either Sigil 'The Internal Tree of the
Roids' or 'Into the Void', depending on which naming
convention you are happy to use.

The Valley lies sunken between two forested sides.
Therefore, upon finding the Valley you should
experience darkness and possibly a feeling of
claustrophobia. There may also be thunderclaps
within the valley, sometimes wet-ones.

If at this point you feel the fear of the unknown
clutching at you then retreat. The Valley is but
the start, once within the Kingdom things get a lot
worse!

At certain cycles the Valley may be flooded with
water. On these occasions you will have to be
very wary, as there may also be floating debris
to contend with.

At all times, flooded or not beware the
Dangleberries. These are the Brown guardians
posted at times by the Kingdoms self defence
mechanisms. To love a Dangleberry, as per loving
a sheep is foolhardy. Dangleberries possess a
hard, crusty, spiky outer shell which can cause
great harm. They also have very sharp teeth. Do
not approach, even though you may be attacked by
their seductive charms. Leave your Velcro gloves
and two-sizes-too-big wellies outside of the
astral.

Many have reported seeing a tree in the Valley: The
Tree of Eyes. The tree is old and weathered. Its
trunk rises to split into two forks, right and left.
The right side has ten eyes, as does the left. In

the main trunk joining the two forks of left-and-right sits a single eye. The tree has moss and fungi growing up its left side, whereas the right side is of clear-white bark. The eyes on the right side are blind. Meditation upon this tree may prove to yield further insights to your true journey within the Kingdom.

The way ahead may be barred by a sealed doorway. The doorway will be set within the face of a mountain and may prove difficult to find, as it may be closed so tight as to just seem a crack upon the mountain face. If you have any doubts, follow your nose.

The doorway will be difficult to open but resolve yourself and will the doorway to open. It is your force of will that shall prove the key.

When opened, may you venture forth into the Kingdom.

The Valley is represented in the physical by the cleft between ones buttocks.

Internal Tree of the Roid Sigil   **Into the Void Sigil**

Plane 1: Dark Cavern

The Dark Cavern is not technically a Plane, though it is the first place you'll venture into within the Kingdom.

The Dark Cavern is simply a large, dark cavern. Its image is that of a prehistoric cave, complete with

wall paintings. The paintings spell-out the history
of the Roid, the first great monkey war and other
such tales of woe.

The paintings also show warnings and caveman
signposts. Take note of the warnings and the
directions. You may find it beneficial to take
with you a large piece of paper and some crayons
(all astrally created). That way you can do a wall
rubbing (in the astral) and thus preserve
direction/warning information (all in the astral
only).

There may be various bones here. Ignore them.

Dark Cavern is represented in the physical by the
rectum opening.

Dark Cavern Sigil

Plane 2: Plane of Fur

The Plane of Fur is, in numerical ordering, the
first true Plane within the Kingdom.

It is a place of incessant hairiness; where the
red sun is obscured by the cactus-like formations
of matted pubic hair.

Beware the cacti! On this Plane you will thirst
like never before but do not stray near the pubic
cacti, for once tangled within their wire-like grip
there is no escape.

It has been fabled that once a great scholar did become stuck upon the pubic cacti. Quick of thought, the scholar created an astral pair of pubic hair-trimmers and thus saved himself from an eternity in the Bush.

You may come across previous travellers within this Plane, travellers entangled within the pubic trap like two pieces of Velcro. DO NOT HELP THEM! They may be real travellers or they may be images created by the Roids, not necessarily Human images too. For example, if within this Plane you come across a little puppy, glassy eyed, looking at you and wagging its tail.... DO NOT attempt to free it. Rather, call the Roids bluff by imagining an astral spear and spear that fucker in the face. That'll show the Roids you are not of simple mind.

If however, you just discover that you've speared another traveller in the face don't worry, run away. Leave them for the Hag. For in the Kingdom of Heme you are by yourself and Mercy must be left far behind you in the Valley of the Scorched.

There is an entity whom has made her home the Plane of Fur: The Hag of Fur. The Hag waits for trapped travellers to die upon the bush then plucks their limp bodies. These she takes to her little cottage and uses them to make all manner of things: curtains, clothes, pots, pans, puppets and Tupperware. Rumour has it that the pubic Cacti may well be constructed from the Hags-own bushy nether-region. It is said that she has been cursed with the ever-blooming bush, a most terrible curse caused by a DIY accident involving a bottle of Miracle Grow. The Hag may approach you but this is rare as she is carrion. Keep your distance from this entity for there are rumours that she is no mere Hag but a witch.

Successfully leaving this Plane shows a control over temptations.

Plane of Fur is represented in the physical by the left buttock.

Plane of Fur Sigil

Plane 3: Plane of Inner Self

The Plane of Inner Self is the most devious of Planes. This Plane will appear as you will it, as your subconscious wills it. Therefore before attempting to venture into this Plane be assured that all you inner-daemons have been fully exorcised.

Whatsoever you may fear, whatsoever you may loathe, and whatsoever embarrassing intimate encounters you may have had, they will all be present within this Plane. Whomsoever shall pass through the Plane of Inner Self unharmed is either a great mage indeed or a fool.

Beware the adverse mental effects that the confrontations on this plane may induce.

I advise that this Plane is avoided until the traveller feels fully satisfied that they are ready to confront themselves.

There was a story about an IT professional, a project manager in fact who decided to enter the astral and, more specifically, the Plane of Inner

Self.

This he did and was presented with his inner
daemons, hidden by his inner desires. The Plane
appeared to him as a server room, filled from
head-to-toe with computers of all sizes and
description. He knew what he was after, and
there it was. The server of the project he'd
just completed, standing a metre above all others
and gleaming like a chrome hubcap. He proceeded
to stick his massive (it was the astral after
all) willy into the server.

When, after a brief moment of biomechanical
cottaging the server, enraptured within its hard
drive-rotating orgasm, promptly toppled down onto
the IT project manager and squashed him flat.

Apparently servers don't much like project
managers, and even less the ones that attempt to
fiddle with them.

Successfully leaving this plane shows calm with
oneself.

Plane of Inner Self is represented in the physical
by the small of the back/lower spine.

Plane of Inner Self Sigil

Plane 4: Plane of Venom

The Plane of Venom is a nasty place to be. The Plane consists of a number of islands suspended within a 360° sphere of Venomous fluid.

As you walk here upon the islands, observe how the liquid reaches up its Venomous paws to strike you in.

You must be strong of mind to leave this Plane alive. For within this Plane normal laws of gravity do not apply and your mind must follow suit. You must, even though there be a sphere of Venom surrounding you, always think that you are walking on the TOP of the island. If for any instance you think that you are walking on the BOTTOM of the island your subconscious will create an instance of schooled impossibility and you shall fall, be it upwards or downwards for direction is irrelevant, to your death.

The Venom if encountered will infect your spirit with a poison, gradually eating you away as a spider digests its prey.

There is a tale of an astute student who boasted about a planned journey to the Plane of Venom. All went well until, halfway through the Plane he allowed himself to think "There is a lake above me and below me, but am I walking on the top of the Island or the underside?". His subconscious, on being presented with such a dilemma reasoned that the whole situation was very silly indeed, and furthermore that it just wasn't going to put up with such silliness anymore.

And so the student fell towards the sky. But, as mentioned this was an astute student and so he quickly blanked his mind and decided that he could fly. Thus it was, with the land at his feet and the lake at his head he floated, pondering on which direction he should take.

The astute student ultimately proved not so astute when, upon deciding his direction of flight he was observed to plunge headfirst into the lake of Venom.

Successfully leaving this Plane shows control of ones thoughts.

Plane of Venom is represented in the physical by the right buttock.

Plane of Venom Sigil

Plane 5: Plane of Fire

The Plane of Fire is the secondary nature of the Roid. Within this Plane, for one whom can stand the intense heat, there is much to be learned about the nature of the Roid.

The heat here will be intense, for the Plane of Fire is a barren land where the great Red Sun beats down continuously.

There is little life on this plane save for the half-rotted Camuel. Camuel's form cannot be described fully in words, except that he, and I can assure you it is a he.... is naked in his rottedness.

Camuel only sustains his existence by draining
the life force of weak-willed travellers. He
will appear as a bent-over rotted old man, with a
reddish-beard and a single horn on his head. You
will be able to recognise Camuel, as he always
appears with seven buckets of water hanging-off
his seven foot erect penis. He also carries
seven drinking straws. And a cock rest (with
wheels).

In the Plane of Fire you will thirst and you will
sweat. Camuel will offer you a bucket of water as
long as you sign a piece of paper stating you will
play a game with him. As soon as you sign your name
a contract will unfold around your signature. The
game is for your life energy. The game is always
Twister and Camuel never looses. Camuel has been
known to allow the choice of a second game to a
disheartened traveller. The second game is as
fatalistic as the first, and shows a cruel side to
Camuel. He will present the traveller with three
rings and then step back ten feet. The traveller
must attempt to throw at least a single ring over
Camuel's seven foot erect penis. The price for
loosing is your life force. The prize for winning is
a goldfish.

Many elders suggest that this second game proves
that Camuel once belonged to a carnival. Possibly
as a stallholder, possibly as a freak.

The Plane of Fire also contains the monuments of the
Ancients. These are massive spherical structures
constructed many thousands of years ago by the
Ancient Roids using captured travellers as slave
labourers. Within these monuments are contained vast
treasures, along with thousands of years of secret

knowledge. Should you venture into an Spheramid beware; the Ancients were cunning and prepared many traps for the unwary.

Apart from Camuel there is also the matter of the Dung Beetles. Also called Dungies, they are an astral perversion of the Earth dung beetle.

The Dungies are well mannered and will give you a drink of water along with interesting conversation. They chat with many travellers and are always eager to pass on the current news of the Kingdom.

However, should they offer you vast treasures in exchange for some dung you must say no. If you say yes, you will be agreeing to a binding agreement for you to fill a small bucket with your dung. Your prize for this will be great treasures.

You will never fill the tiny bucket.

The crafty Dungies have anchored a wormhole to the bottom of the bucket; any dung you produce will be whisked-away to the Dungies deep subterranean lair. Your dung will go straight to their King who never fills, thus all you produce will amount (in substance) to nought. Should you try to break the agreement then the Dungies will, by the power of their astral control suck you down the tiny bucket. You will become a prisoner of the Dungies and you will be force fed prunes and strapped to the tiny bucket, forced to spend an eternity crapping without a newspaper.

Successfully leaving this Plane shows control of cravings.

Plane of Fire is represented in the physical by just above the left hip.

Plane of Fire Sigil

Plane 6: Plane of Stench

Beware the fumes within the Plane of Stench, for they will send you into madness.

The Plane of Stench was not always so. It used to be the Plane of Little Kittens.

However, Raymond Small, a greedy Orang-utan had his spirit banished to the Plane of Little Kittens after he ate the Gigantic Banana (constructed for the coming of Munky) and imploded, thus creating Africa.

Raymond was a resident of the Plane of Little Kittens for no more than a day when its name had to be changed. Raymond in his greed had eaten all of the kittens.

Raymond stayed upon this Plane eating all that ventured forth, even Roids. He became so large that his titty mass now forms the ground of the Plane of Stench, so called because his anus had grown to the size of Australia. And when your arse is Australia, it lets out one hell of a pong.

Every hour of the day Stavros, the spirit of a man possessed by the Roid, ventures forth into the Plane of Stench with his chemically sealed kebab van. Here, within his chemical warfare suit he feeds Raymond fifty king size kebabs with extra chilli sauce. This is a dangerous task, for often does Raymond try to tempt Stavros into his gaping jaws.

In his greed Raymond doesn't realise that by eating the man who feeds him, he would infact be killing himself.

Beware the Chilli Sauce of Stavros. Only the lead-lined gullet of Raymond can withstand such a potent sauce. Be careful where you step, for pools of chilli sauce litter the Plane of Stench. If you step in one of these your foot will be digested by the living sauce. However, if you possess a lead-lined vessel and are very careful, you could scoop up some chilli sauce for it would make a deadly weapon.

The Plane of Stench looks like a volcano range and, to some extent that is what it is. As the years have passed there is actually very little titty mass forming the ground of the Plane. Most of the ground, and indeed the volcano formations you will see are formed of a hardened top crust of orang utan dung. The problem is drainage. There is none, so Raymond, unable to move is actually sitting within a hardened shell of his own faeces. Underneath the hardened top layer the excrement is still quite squidgy. Because of this, the landmass of the Plane of Stench has been observed getting higher. This is due to the build-up of fresh dung down below, pushing the hardened layer ever upwards.

To this effect Heme has instructed drainage to be prepared, as the rise of dung will have two effects:

1)   Raymond will drown in his own poo. Heme doesn't really care about this happening; Stavros is bleeding him dry in kebab costs to keep the fat monkey alive.

2)   The Plane of Stench will become blocked.

Drainage used to be fine within this Plane. Raymond sits within a giant porcelain bathtub. One fateful day Raymond Small was fiddling with his tiny cock whilst seated in the bathtub and managed to get it stuck in the plughole (along with his ginger ballsack). For years he has struggled to free himself. Raymond is now so encrusted within his bathtub that he cannot move. There is a plan to drill-up the drain and through the plug hole itself. However, finding volunteers for this shit work is proving difficult, for it would surely be an action of suicide.

The fumes of this ever-shifting dung spurts out of the volcanoes so, when traversing this Plane it is always wise to carry a gas mask. Breathing-in the noxious fumes would dissolve your insides instantly. Contact with your skin would be as acid; stay wrapped up.

However there is a bigger threat.

Raymond, though now unable to move still has his persuasive manner aswell as his greed.

He will try and trick you by feigning illness. To this extent he may pretend he has something stuck within his teeth. He will probably promise you treasures if you help him. After this, if you still ignore his requests he will threaten legal action against you. Ignore him. Raymond is an arse hole driven by greed. He will never change. Even when he chokes upon his own filth will he suffer no reflection of his life spent in the pursuit of greed. The green-eyed monster has no mercy.

He will also try and trick you by mimicking other

voices. His favourite is to mimic a small baby crying. He uses these different voices to draw unwary travellers to his jaws.

Make haste through this Plane.

However, it is written that if favour can be gained from Raymond he will speak of hidden treasures. There are two ways to make favour with a greedy orang utan buried in his own stinking faeces:

1)   By scratching any itch he may have upon his vast titty mass. For this you will require an astral gardening rake.

2)   By jumping down his throat and becoming his next meal.

Of the two options, option number one tends to find favour amongst most sane people.

There was a tale of a traveller who, fuelled by deviousness dropped a handful of cod liver oil capsules into Raymond's mouth. Raymond ate them without question and the traveller ran off before the eruptions could begin...

There is also a tale, again involving students, of students who attempted to set up a bungee jumping business within the Plane of Stench. The idea was that travellers would pay to bungee jump down Raymond's pothole-like gullet. Upon the day of opening they were duly shutdown: they had misjudged the lengths of cord to be used.

Successfully leaving this Plane shows strength of character.

Plane of Stench is represented in the physical by just above the right hip.

Plane of Stench Sigil

Plane 7: Plane of Pleasure

To move through the Plane of Pleasure you must invert the Plane. Therefore, speed of movement within this Plane is governed by Pain. The more pain you suffer, the greater your movement within.

However, the task will not be easy. Each notion of Pleasure you experience will drive you backwards, away from your goal.

Temptation will be great here. You will be surrounded by fit birds (or blokes if you're a lady or a gay) that will attempt to undress you, kiss you, touch you and put things in their mouths.

RESIST RESIST!! If you succumb to these charms then your journey will end here; you will never return to your body.

To move forward you must cause yourself deep pain. I'd recommend a ballsack clamp (astral) for blokes (or testosterone-charged women) or something similar for the ladies (setting pretty cushions on fire perhaps?).

Successfully leaving this Plane shows control and suppression of emotion.

Plane of Pleasure is represented in the physical by the left armpit.

Plane of Pleasure Sigil

Plane 8: Plane of Pain

To move through the Plane of Pain you must invert
the Plane. Therefore, speed of movement within this
Plane is governed by Pleasure. The more pleasure
you suffer, the greater your movement within.

However, the task will not be easy. Each notion of
Pain you experience will drive you backwards, away
from your goal.

Temptation will be great here. You will be
surrounded by old birds (or blokes if you're a lady
or a gay) that will attempt to undress you, kiss
you, touch you and put things in their mouths.

RESIST RESIST!! If you succumb to these charms
then your journey will end here; you will never
return to your body.

To move forward you must cause yourself deep
pleasure. I'd recommend sex with a famous
Australian pop-singer (astral) for blokes (or
lesbo's) or something similar for the ladies (sewing
perhaps?).

Successfully leaving this Plane shows control
and suppression of emotion.

Plane of Pain is represented in the physical by the right armpit.

Plane of Pain Sigil

Plane 9: Palace of Heme

This is Hemes Palace. No living soul has reached the Palace and returned intact to provide a description (my own journey there has been blocked-out by my subconscious). Needless to say it is the abode of Heme himself, king of the Roids.

The Palace of Heme is surrounded by a great wall a hundred metres high. The wall was built despite protests from the Kingdom of a humanitarian concern. Though seeking to protect the Palace, the wall actually imprisons the Kingdom.

Evil affording the luxury of keeping Evil away.

Legend states that Heme employs four daemon bodyguards, so beware. These bodyguards are an unknown fixture, but legend hints that they may be the spirits of the first Badgers driven underground by a conformist world. If so, these would be very angry badgers. As a mark of loyalty to Heme, it is rumoured that the Badgers have sworn an oath of non-copulation. This oath has meant that their hairy striped ball sacks have grown to an enormous size, making walking impossible. The Badgers, upon applying lube down the front of their testiculae are able to push themselves along with their extended arms. Thus they have become a living Space Hopper, but more hairy. This sliding motion makes the Badgers very fast and very silent: as the Ninjas of old they are able to approach their prey unawares. It also saves on buying shoes, though it makes negotiating stairs an impossibility.

The Badgers maintain testicle pressure by the use of a Testicle Applied Pressure device, or a TAP. The TAP is really their only weakness (except for stairs). If you can open the TAP and deflate the striped gonads you will render the Badger immobile. Although if you get this close to a Badger you're in real trouble. The Badgers can also use the TAP to release pressure within their testiculae for journeys over rough terrain. They also use the TAP as a source of lube, and for washing their fur.

Never shake hands with a Badger.

You will also have to contend with Heme's Hairy Green Turtle.

Although Heme has ultimate sovereign power over his kingdom, there are a few political parties who fight for governing power. The party is chosen by the people, though Heme has the last say on all things within the Kingdom including who governs. The three main parties are:

1) The Blue Party. Members of this party are in the large a bunch of closed-door bummers who delight in sexual perversity and fetish spanking. Their policies demand action and generally are favoured by Heme himself, though some of the leaked details of the parties sexual misconducts have sickened even him. Members attending dinner parties

have been reported to have 'jockey' events: half pretend to be jockeys and half pretend to be horses, whereupon the jockeys jump onto the horses and are carried around the dining table amid hoots of screaming, the clinking of stirrups and the chaffing of nipple-reigns. The jockeys are kept erect upon the backs of the 'horses' only by the determined anal clenching of their steeds. Tally ho! Indeed.

2) The Red Party. This party tries to be friends to all people, avoids confrontations and always smiles at you. A big patronising smile pillared by ears the size of midgets. But beware the smile; for it is the smile of the Crocodile. This party lies like a bastard. Everything that comes out of their festering mouths stinks like auntie Mable's knickers on a bad day. Even Heme has hired an army of lawyers to scribe-through the finer points of their policies, for many a time have they tried to screw the Kingdom and its loyal subjects. This party is most expensive to run, the people hate it (though are often deceived by Mr. Smiley-face with living midget-ears and his pantomime-cow with dyslexic mouth wife), and the party makes the public pay for its members benefits, like fat bastards being granted four public-funded houses, and corrupt MPs who wallow in their 'necessary' expense claims whilst the rest of the Kingdom goes hungry. It would seem that their Home Secretary is blind to his people and their needs. All this and still the people vote favourably. What will be the downfall of this gravy train? A war perhaps to deface the multi-

faceted leather-eared Crocodile... Or a cabinet that can no longer have their lies spun?

3) The Yellow Party. Members of this party spend all their time moaning. They complain that the people should be more environmentally friendly, that love is the answer to crime, that all the young should have their wages taken away and given to the old, that economic migration into the Kingdom should be encouraged, that the rights of criminals take precedence over the rights of society, that over sixty's should be given free contraceptives, that under fourteens should be given free-babies etc. etc. All they do is fucking moan. So much time is spent on moaning and on 'Ghost' policies that little or (as is mostly the case) no action is ever taken. The members stand around with their cocks in their hands (or lady-lips, if a lady or a fully-converted tranny), moaning and moaning but not actually doing anything. The people of the Kingdom love this party for after the election, their huge policy documents are distributed amongst the people to be used as toilet roll. The party can therefore be said of all the parties, to be doing the most to clean up the Kingdom.

Palace of Heme is represented in the physical by the base of the neck/top of the spine.

Hidden Planes

There has long been rumour of Hidden Planes
existing within the Kingdom. These hidden Planes
are found by traversing ancient paths which have
become downtrodden, almost unwalkable.

Also, as nothing is known of these Planes they could
be much more dangerous than any presented here
within this book of my travels. Remember, the
Kingdom of Heme is a corruption of the Kingdom
wherein Go(r)d sits; the Original Kingdom created by
his imagination: the Kingdom of Haven.

Heme has taken the power of Go(r)d's subconscious
and used it to create a mirror of the Kingdom of
Haven. And as the mirror reverses, thus the Kingdom
is.

There is a fabled Plane of Bad Fortune which has
been recorded within the Internal Body of
Magicians (IBM) thus:

The Plane is said to have been discovered by an
astute student. The student travelled there and,
upon his return painted a vivid description of the
Plane. Apparently the Plane is a vast ocean of bogs
and marshes, into which lightning crashes
continuously and pink Whale-Frogs mate noisily.

The astute student, wanting to prove himself more
astute than his astute peers, ventured forth into

the Plane wearing nothing more than a plastic
snorkel and a pair of copper swimming trunks.

Observers back at the university said his body
lit up and smoked like a very badly wired set of
Christmas tree lights.

Needless to say he didn't return to his body in
the state that he left. For the rest of his
elongated life he had to live carrying the defect
of impotency.

So the morale here is to beware. Always be prepared
for the worst and never, ever find it necessary to
undress into a pair of copper swimming trunks. Not
even in your home where you think no one will see.
But what's that, your net curtains aren't quite
opaque enough? Mrs Rogers from number 23 has just
seen you flashing your copper-crusted groin about
and has ran down to the grocers screaming, her eyes
awash with tears? And what will you do when the
villagers surround your house and force you out of
the village, not before administering a good kicking
and swimming-trunk reshaping with extra-strong
magnets? What then?

When you're booted out of your village and the next
village turns you away in disgust, unable as you
were to remove the magnet-misshapen copper swimming
trunks from your person, the copper deformities now
intensely wrapped around your ball-sack like a habit
around a nun? What then? You'll probably kill
yourself, or get struck by lightning. Either way:
IT'S NOT WORTH IT. Also it's worth remembering that
copper swimming trunks will, eventually, make your
nob go blue.

There is also rumour of a vast Red ocean Plane,
populated by mysterious creatures including scuba-

diving Gnomes and half-fish, half-Unicorn entities. It is rumoured that the Red sun of the Kingdom sets into the ocean within this Plane, boiling all living creatures. The creatures are created again at Dawn the next day, ready for the same cycle. Wise men say that this Plane must be ruled by a memory-repeater subconcious bubble, like a Flashback.

Also beware the lower passages that frequent the Kingdom. These passages have almost all fallen into disuse and are now rumoured to contain the remnants of astral travellers gone mad.

Half human, half tomato they are rumoured to roam the Kingdoms subterranean caves and tunnels in search of more astral travelers, for these beings have turned cannibal.

Many say it's the madness that drives these entities. Others say they got lost and were either driven mental or had their physical bodies destroyed.

The most wise think that it's a case of the tomato getting payback against the fruit-fiddlers. For the Tomato is like an elephant: even in passing it never forgets.

There is also a rumour that within the deepest tunnels of the Kingdom lies the Tomato Graveyard, a place where old tomatoes come to die. It is rumoured to be as a vast mountain, constructed from the seeds of those tomatoes whom have rotted away. Show respect if you shall encounter the Tomato Graveyard upon your travels, for the departed tomato souls are easy to anger.

The Stream Of Ages

Throughout the Kingdom there runs a stream. This is
the Stream of Ages. The stream starts off small,
shallow of depth and narrow of girth, though always
fast-flowing across an abundance of shiny pebbles.
After a while the stream expands both in depth and
in girth; the current slowing so as to make the
stream seem a huge lake; pebbles and rocks becoming
immersed within the blackness of the water. But
soon the stream again narrows. Thinner and thinner
it becomes, shallower and shallower are its waters.
And soon the pebbles disappear to nought, as does
the water. Though you may follow this stream you
must pray never to reach its ending, for this would
be the end of all things.

Though many have tried, none have found the
source of this Stream of Ages. It would seem as
though the stream emerged from nought, and
returns thus at its closure.

The Fountain of Dis Pleasure

It is rumoured that within the Kingdom lies a
fountain. This fountain spurts forth no ordinary
display however; it is said to contain the Elixir of
Eternal Youth.

The fountain is difficult to find, if even it
exists! You will know that you have found the
fountain whence you come upon a three-legged
structure of perfect black stone. The fountain is
engraved thus: Savour The Universes Power In Drink.

The promise of the fountain is true in a sense.
However it should be noted that the Elixir does not
revert youth in the flesh: indeed what use would

such a potion have within the world of the Astral?
Could one ever such exist at all? The Elixir
regresses mental age.

Be wary to drink with caution, and even then a
mere sip should suffice. The Elixir has been known
to regress travellers back even to pre-feotal
states of mental awareness. All you have learned
will be vanquished.

To search for such everlasting youth is a folly
pursued only by mankind. Anti-Aging products adorn
the shelves of the many. Aging is part of the
beautiful cycle of biological life [and death]: it
is not ours to change.

Whether Dis is a corruption of This, as practised by
modern language students, is a hotly debated
subject. In the same way that bottle often
embarrassingly becomes bockle. What the fuck is a
bockle? I don know nuffin bout dis shit.

The Waterfall of Dreams

There is, for those of wit enough to find it a
waterfall within the Kingdom that stands a mighty
three hundred and thirty three feet high. This
waterfall cascades into a black pool which, though
pounded by the falling water only ever shows a
faint ripple across its surface.

The waterfall has been called the Waterfall of
Dreams due to the images seen by travellers within
its falling waters. These images are refractions
of all the colours of the spectrum, as light broken
by a prism.

These images are conceptions: some say dreams,

others say ideas. They live for a brief period during their fall downwards towards the black pool of still water. As they hit the pool-surface they are enveloped by the blackness; they become part of it: part of nothing, of no thing.

Most do not cause any disturbance upon the surface of the black pool when they hit, they are absorbed as energy spent and tired. However some do. A single ripple, a single resonance before extinction. And these ripples travel outwards to the circular banks of the pool, whereupon they leave their mark. Not all can at first see these marks, these tiny displacements of soil and mud upon the large pool-bank but they are there.

They exist for those who want to see.

The Holy Mountain

Through your journeys you may come across the Holy Mountain. The summit of this mountain is said to contain a richness of knowledge uncomprehensible by human imagination. To climb to the summit you must pass through a gateway of two apple trees. Though you will hunger for these apples weigh down not your pockets with sin, for once you reach the summit you shall be judged.

General Notes

Beware the thorned plant that yields the fruit which you desire, for when reaching for this fruit you may prick yourself.

Also beware the small trees bearing the berries of Red. You may notice that as you pass the branches

sway in unison, almost as if they were following
you. Know that they are following you! These
trees are the eyes of Heme, and are plentiful
within the Kingdom. As the ancient Egyptians used
black water to skry, so has Heme his trees of Red.

There is an entity within the forested parts of the
Kingdom that you should be wary of. Her name is
Denise and she is the spirit of the forest itself.
She appears along country-paths as a female jogger,
fit of form and active of libido. She will talk to
you and try and entice you to have sex with her.
Resist! Sex will enslave you to this spirit: you
will be turned into a Squirrel and be tasked with
gathering Acorns so that the forest may grow.

Grey squirrels are male: Red ones female. From this
we can deduce that more men than women would have
sex with a female complete stranger.

The Etheric Octopus

Rumour would also have us believe that the Planes of
the Kingdom are suspended upon the tentacles of a
giant, sleeping octopus. This octopus is part of
the psychic Ether, and thus conveniently he has
never been seen. The Octopus' enormous testicles
act like a huge anchor, keeping it and the Kingdom
in one place.

It is said that the Etheric Octopus secretes an
electrical discharge into the Kingdom. Roid
scholars aswell as astral travellers have long
pondered where this source comes from. Some reckon
it's natural radiation from the Octopus' decomposing
matter. Others say it's discharges from the
Octopus' mind. There are some less-kind theories
too, but these are not for here. The first idea,

that of decomposition has met with the greatest exceptance. However, it has also caused the most fear, for if the octopus did decompose then what would keep the Kingdom moored within the Ether? To calm fears there has been another theory put-forward. To moor the great Octopus against the strong Etheric currents it's testicles would have to be immense. Aswell as being able to anchor the huge body mass, they would have to be much more dense to combat the effects of Etheric currents against surface area [of the Octopus]. Therefore, either the Octopus sports a pair of bollocks bigger than its body (which would probably prohibit mating), or its testiculae are not of fleshy-matter.

The Council Of Roid Public Sciences and Esoteric Studies (or C.O.R.P.S.E.S), suggest that the Octopus has balls made of brass. This would provide the mass necessary for anchorage, and may also account for the Kingdoms three suns (one true sun reflecting light off the two brass testicles).

Roid engineers are current constructing a huge electromagnet to lower and attach to the brass bollocks. This will provide an anchor if the theory that the Octopus is rotting proves to be true. Building the magnet is not a problem, though it is a mammoth task. Finding where to lower the magnet is a problem not yet addressed by C.O.R.P.S.E.S members.

If the Octopus turns out to be a female who just got stuck somewhere, then the magnet idea won't work and in time the Kingdom may cease to threaten mankind.

It is said that if this electrical energy could be harnessed then the Kingdom could live forever with clean, free energy. At the moment most of the

Kingdoms power is provided by mining the Plane of Stench.

There are three main problems with this power source:

1)   It really smells bad. Like a locked room full of old people

2)   Raymond's excrement is extremely toxic

3)   It really is a shit job.

At least the mining is subterranean in operation. Raymond's verbal shite is much more deadly than his physical ginger-basted shite.

One Roid known as Alset did invent such a device for tapping this ambient electrical source. However, the Kingdom's fuel corporations didn't want to diminish either their hold on the Kingdom or their profits, and so Aslet was 'dealt with'. All of his genius work was confiscated by Heme's Red Bureau of Investigation (RBI) and was locked away within his private libraries. Alsets studies have never been released, the fuel corporations have seen to that. Even under the Freedom of Information act these documents are kept quite secret. The Freedom of Information act was passed to allow the Roids a window into their governments operation, and to force the government to account for their actions. Funny then how the government conducted an unmonitored purge just before the act was passed as Law.

The RBI is known to have links with a powerful commercial body within the Kingdom; the Used Salesman Association. Links between the Used Salesman Association and control of the Kingdoms fuel supplies have all but been proven. For personal greed they fuck the people.

The coming of the Octopus has remained a mystery, although his mass has effectively plugged the hole in the Kingdom's Ozone layer. Many use this fact to justify the claim that the Octopus was sent by Gord. Others claim the Octopus is merely a good samaritan.

Naturalists however, use calendars to claim that the Octopus was actually in heat: his desperation leading to his 'mating' with the Kingdom. They claim that this pent-up sexual matter would explain the enormous size of his gonads.

Though no one is able to explain why they are made of brass.

Of The Spitting Cobra

From time to time there appears within the heavens of The Kingdom a phenomenon which the scholars of The Kingdom have yet to explain.

For a matter of minutes there appears within the skies a huge elongated mass bearing a single, angry eye. This beast appears to shuffle in and out of The Kingdom before pausing to cry white-hot tears of coconut juice upon the startled observers watching the spectacle unfold.

A theory generally accepted by the masses is that, like the Etheric Octopus, the Spitting Cobra is searching the vast Etheric Ocean for something lost. Quite what this 'lost' item is no-one knows, though the finest Roid scholar has proposed that the Cobra is infact searching for a giant wicker basket.

As for the tears well, most agree that due to the frequency of the Cobras visit to The Kingdom that it must be traveling in circles. When the Cobra realises this it starts crying — realising that its search is progressing no-where.

Two things are certain of the Cobra.

The first is that the visits by the Cobra to the Kingdom have been getting more and more frequent as years go by.

The second is that the Cobra seems to change the colour of its skin based on season.

Description Of The Most Terrible Roids

There are a number of different 'species' of Roid.

They are Lesser Roids, Greater Roids, the Hairy Green Turtle and of course, Heme.

Strictly speaking the Turtle isn't a Roid. However, the Turtle only exists within the Kingdom of the Roid and is under the command of Heme. Heme himself is higher than all Roids; he is the Avatar Massive.

It must be said that in the physical world, the Roids are very limited as to their appearance. For example, they can only manifest as stationary red-grapes. However, within the Kingdom the Roids may take any form they see fit. If you see a Roid within the Kingdom you are probably looking at an image generated half by the Roid and half by your own interpretation/expectancy. The Astral nature of the Kingdom makes this happen. Strictly speaking, in the Astral you see what you want to see. Hence the appearance of the Roid is shared between your 'minds eye' and the Roid, who is actually just a projection onto the Astral themself.

This does make clearer the stories of astral travellers becoming seduced by the Roids. Being seduced by a Red grape is silly however, as explained above the Red berry in the astral can appear quite beautiful. One thing to note is that Roids will always appear with a reddish skin. This is because Roids obtain the majority of their power from Red, with the rest being obtained from person's belief and from the letter R. They could, in theory change the colour of their skin but they would thus be loosing much of their 'self', or being.

Of the Lesser Roids

The Lesser Roids are great in number but weak in strength. They are not covered by this magical tome because they are not important. The Lesser Roids may prove a very slight discomfort but they are never going to affect mankind. Lesser Roids appear as Pimples, Spots and Zits. There is also a Higher-Lesser Roid whom materialises as a Boil.

Lesser Roids are often used by Heme to maintain a 'hook' into the physical world of man. Without the Lesser Roids Heme would have to re-open the gateway each time he wanted to transgress the astral and enter out into the physical. Opening the gate is very difficult. Time contributes to this level of difficulty. Therefore, if man were able to eradicate all Spots, Pimples, Zits and Boils from the Earth, then Heme would have a problem.

Fortunately for Heme mankind has bred its own Lesser Roid receptacle in the form of the Teenager. This grease monkey entity provides the exacting environment needed for Lesser Roid habitation: lots of grease and adversity to having a bath.

Generally Lesser Roids do not cause too much distress to Humans. This is due to their subservient duties: they must sit and avoid attention and thus preventative measures being taken, all the while keeping the physical gateway open for their master, Heme.

If you are afflicted with the Lesser Roid then you must take measures to cleanse the scum from your surface. By being passive in these matters you are assisting Heme in his goals. In this instance

putting a bag over your head won't help, even if
you do cut-out eye holes.

Of the Hairy Green Turtle

The Hairy Green Turtle is a Golem of sorts.
Animated by Heme for his own uses, the Turtle is
almost indestructible.

Heme shall sit astride his Hairy Green Turtle upon
his coming and subsequent assault upon mankind.
The Turtle will carry him onwards upon its
indestructible hide, absorbing enemies as they may
come before him.

The Turtle is made of shit. Not any old poop, it
has to be Green, for Green is where it derives most
of its power. The Greener the better. Non-green
specimens seem to fall-apart upon animation. Also
it has to be Hairy. The more Hairy the better and
the more indestructible the Turtle is. The Hairs
seem to run through the Turtles body, holding it
together like the steel girders within reinforced
concrete.

Once Heme has a suitable specimen he holds it within
his Palace, feeding it with Roids and foolish astral
travellers that venture into his domain. Thus the
turtle grows from a tiny piece of poop into a
monster.

For the animation process Heme entraps the spirit of
his mother-in-law within the terrible turd and binds
her to his service. Thus the Turtle is a ferocious
beast, a beast who left unguarded openly attacks all
and sundry. Fearless, the Turtle is more than a
match for all, except of course the Astral Baby.

The Turtle attacks by three main methods:

1)   The Turtle crushes its enemy under its
        huge body mass. This is probably the
        best way to go when confronted by this
        monster.

2)   The Turtle absorbs its prey into its
        body mass where it will be slowly
        digested. This attack is very nasty:
        the absorption process takes quite long
        and is extremely painful and smelly.
        Anyone caught off-guard and thus
        absorbed by the Turtle serves to add to
        its body mass.

3)   Probably the worst attack is the
        Turtles Psychic Nag. Even if you do
        escape the Turtle, the echoes of the
        Psychic Nag will remain with you
        forever. The Psychic Nag is used by
        the Turtle to wear-down prey before a
        strike. It is said that there is no
        preventative measure for the Nag: it
        even penetrates a lead-lined helmet.

The Turtle can, when encountered upon the Astral
present herself in any form. Due to the nature of
the Turtle, you will most likely encounter the
Turtle as a twenty-one year old Goddess, usually
draped in nothing more than a bikini. See past
this illusion if you favour your life. See past
the perfect skin and into the wrinkles awash with
Oil of Ulay. See past the firm, pert breasts into
the saggy lumps that hang from the old hags armpits
like sacks of coal. See past the toned thighs into
the mottled, map-of-the-M25 chicken legs beyond.
If you can do this then you may have time to turn
on your heels and run. Do not let her get

intimate, for her Velcro-lined upper-lip and living bush will attach and not let go; you will be absorbed like the other unfortunates who choose to part grannies curtains.

The Turtle has also been known to appear as a nine-headed hydra (mainly to female travellers). In the form of the nine-headed hydra, the Psychic Nag is magnified nine-fold.

There is a question outstanding from this examination of the Turtle: Hemes wife.

There is, within the confines of the history of the Universe, no record of Heme ever being married. However, the nature of the Turtle (animated via the spirit of his mother-in-law) dictates that he is married.

All information concerning Hemes wife has only come-about from the rumours of scholars; people said to have entered the Palace and left with their bits intact.

Hemes wife is imprisoned within the Palace. Her cell has been made-up as an art studio and she spends her days making sculptures from liver and onion pate. She has to be gagged at all times for her piercing squeal of a voice can make a man's hair fall out (hence why Heme is himself quite, quite bald). Her voice has also been known to kill birds, large and small. She seems to have quite a knack at directing her voice towards a specific target. She can pluck a specific bird from the sky at fifty-yards and more.

Her voice wasn't always this bad. It used to be sweet and soft until she found out Heme was having an affair with Munky. From that day Heme has ordered her to be gagged, lest she use her voice against him.

It also stops her from trying to talk about
football.

Of the Greater Roids

The Greater Roids are those which manifest as the fiery grapes. Within the Kingdom Greater Roids are used by Heme to patrol the Tunnels Major, and to deal with any unwanted travellers.

The Greater Roids, unlike the lesser Roids are much harder to deal with. Their physical manifestation causes great distress to their host.

There are documented ways of dealing with the Greater Roids in the physical (as explained later), but to deal with them in the Astral is another matter. Your best weapon is avoidance. Second best weapon: a swift pair of legs.

Each Greater Roid has been combined with the spirit of an elemental force, which is why they are so powerful. The elemental force is subservient to the Roid, until called forth (usually when the Roid is in a state of aggression). The four different types of elements are Air, Fire, Water and Earth. Heme is the only Roid to have successfully combined with all four elemental forces, hence why he is king.

Here is a list of those Greater Roids that I know about. There is certain to be more, but these are the primary Roids: the guardians of the gateways. I have written here all that I now know of them.

HIDEE AOS

Hidee Aos is the most beautiful of the Greater Roids. Her hair (or 'his hair'; if you are a lady or a gay) flows in golden locks that capture the essence of the Red Sun of the Kingdom.

Dressed in a bikini she will awe you. Speaking with a voice as soft as non-iced snow she will seduce you unto her charms. She usually appears with a bunch of baby rabbits and sits on her knees, playing with them. All this is a deception.

Hidee Aos is rotten inside.

If you fall under her spell then for you there is no hope. Only a mirror can reveal the true nature of Hidee Aos, for as the reflection reverses so too shall it unmask this creature.

Hidee Aos will insist that you run your fingers through her long, golden, flowing hair. Beware, for her hair will slice you to the bone as razor wire. Armless, you shall become helpless.

If you avoid her hair then Hidee Aos will attempt to seduce you into sucking her left big toe. Beware, for her left big toe contains a stinging barb, as the sting of the Wasp. The barb administers a potent chemical, which will leave you helpless.

If you resist the left big toe sucking then she will pressure you to suck the big toe of her right foot. Beware, for her right toe is even more dangerous than the left! Her right big toe is as a snake and, upon sucking it will slither down your throat and eat you from the inside out.

If you resist both toes then she will insist that you lick her belly button. Beware, for her belly button is a wormhole disguised and, upon your moisture will suck you into a bottomless well, where you will fall for eternity and a day (which, when considered is an impossible quasi-time concept). If the belly button doesn't do it for you then she'll get her baps out, playing with them under the

Red Sun. She'll tempt you to suck her nipples. Beware, for her nipples are coated with an epoxy-resin and, as soon as you've clamped-on you'll be stuck. Her nipple will then start to expel compressed air into your lungs. At this point one of her cute little bunny's will have jumped up you arse-hole, thus creating an airtight seal. Your eyes will pop-out and, eventually you will explode. Before exploding you may be one of the unfortunate ones who gets to obtain the cock they've always dreamed of... Builds you-up then makes you explode.

If you aren't a very big practitioner of foreplay then Hidee Aos will get down to business. After a dance of seduction (accompanied by the music of Agado) she will rip her kit-off and pull you close, pushing your head down, ever downwards unto her nether-region. Do not get too close to her fanny! It is as a giant Venus Fly trap and, if captured by its lusty lure then you will be dissolved within the internal acids of Hidee Aos.

If you resist all this then Hidee Aos will offer to depart, after you have administered her with a kiss. Beware, for this is the worst trick! On kissing her you will instantly feel her slip her tongue-in, as Grandma used to do at Christmas.... But that's not the worst, oh no! As she gets more passionate you will feel her stubble, and you will feel her stubble begin to rip at your face. And you'd be correct in your feelings... Her stubble is like tungsten-tipped screws and will shred your poor face from your body.

In the physical Hidee Aos takes a more literal approach. The red-berry of Hidee Aos is the most horrible you will ever see.

You have been warned!

Hidee Aos is of Earth.

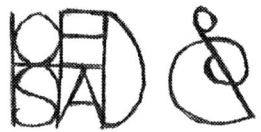

Hidee Aos Sigil and Seal

FIN DAAPOL

Fin Daapol is an odd character. He appears as an old man, bent double and carrying what appears to be a twin-pronged walking stick. He will initiate conversation with you about many things: the Kingdom, the outside world, your career etc. Upon meeting him he seems like an old, slightly mad old man. He even has a one-eyed dog with only three legs and a huge pair of bollocks.

Fin Daapol will always bring the conversation round to dowsing and he will brag that he can find a pool anywhere with the aid of his walking stick, which is really a dowsing rod. If you show interest in his claims then he will offer a demonstration of his skills. He will grasp the rod and set-off with his dog in tow, beckoning you to follow.

After a while he will stop suddenly, his dowsing rod pointing to the ground and hosting an excited smirk upon his crusty old face. He will exclaim that he has found a spring at the end of his rod. He will produce a spade from under his robes and start to dig. Though an old man he will make headways very quickly in his digging.

After some time he will start to complain of back trouble and will ask you to take over. At this point you must ask yourself the question do you really want to find a spring at all?

Being the gentleman (or gentlelady) that you are, you will offer to help the old man. As you dig the dog will take a position facing you, lying down at the edge of your earthen-hole. The dog will start to lick its huge pair of bollocks.

At first you will find this action funny: embarrassing even.

However, the action will start to hypnotise you. Soon you will be in a trance and will not realise just how deep you have dug your hole.

With a snap of his fingers Fin Daapol will bring you out of the trance. He will only do this when you have dug deep enough to trap yourself. The time this process takes is variable dependent upon soil-matter. It has been known to take several years upon really hard ground.

Your pleas for help will come to nought as Fin Daapol, perched on the edge of the hole starts to fill it with a spring, the water of which shall start spurting from the end of his dowsing rod. You will drown within your own hole as the old man looks on; his dog still lay on the edge licking its enormous bollocks.

You see, when the old man told you there was a spring at the end of his rod he wasn't lying...

It is rumoured that the old man is afraid of solid food, and if you confront him with such he will jump astride his three-legged dog and ride (stumble) away.

Fin Daapol is of Water.

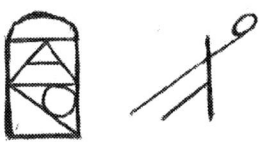

Fin Daapol Sigil and Seal

ME DUPSA

Me Dupsa is an old-fashioned Roid in that she doesn't use any tricks or disguises to extinguish unwanted travellers.

Me Dupsa appears as a seven-headed red dragon-lady. No tricks here: Me Dupsa will kill you in the old-fashioned way.

If Me Dupsa has any weakness, it would be that she has succumbed to the old adage that two heads are better than one, and therefore seven heads are better than two by a factor of three-point-five.

Three-point-five is an interesting number. It is neither three nor four, but in the middle. Three-point-five is the number of anuses that Me Dupsa has: one shared between each pair of heads, with the half-anus belonging to the middle head.

It is a common rumour that three of Me Dupsa's heads are Lesbians and three are straight, with the seventh (middle) head acting as referee.

Me Dupsa is of Fire.

Me Dupsa Sigil and Seal

DIDAPOOH

Didapooh is a most unfortunate Roid. Cursed with a slack colon he travels the Kingdom begging for clean pants from travellers.

He is the one Roid who really isn't that dangerous. He will ask you for a clean set of underwear and, if you say no he will become quite angry and will attack you with his rock-hard brown club.

Didapooh is a very large Roid and so it isn't in your best interests to get into a fight with him. However, he is easy to outrun, since the gigantic log in his underpants means he has to tread very carefully!

Always be wary of your surroundings however. Didapooh is quite aware of his weaknesses and will probably have set-up an ambush site. Know that if you meet Didapooh it is because he wanted you to meet him.

A trick he employs is to cover your escape-route with skid marks, thus making you slide and fall over, allowing Didapooh to crash his club on your head.

It is written that Didapooh can be bribed by offering him some toilet paper, in return for safe passage. He also has affections for toilet air-

freshener, the sort he can hang down the insides of
his underpants.

Didapooh is of Earth.

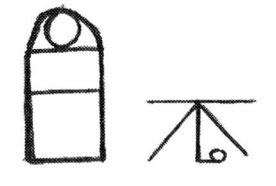

Didapooh Sigil and Seal

FIREST ARTOR

This Roid is a nut. He really is crazy.

Firest Artor likes matches. Specifically he
likes them because they can be used to start
fires.

Do not even approach this Roid. He appears dressed
as a nun and looking quite harmless. However, if
you approach so that you can see his flattened nose,
stubble-soaked chin and toothless grin then you have
approached too closely.

Under his habit Firest Artor keeps his special
'home brew' in corked glass bottles. These he
will reveal to you just as he lights the taper
and throws it.

Firest Artor has no known weaknesses, though he
does like to show off with party tricks, all
involving burning various parts of his body. If
you can entice him into showing you these party
tricks then that will buy you some time to think.

Think fast though, for as soon as he's finished burning his body he will start to burn yours.

In the physical, Firest Artor will burn your ring.

Firest Artor is of Fire.

Firest Artor Sigil and Seal

LOOK ILIK EBEEVER

Look Ilik Ebeever is a hairy Roid. Oft you will not see the Roid within: just a mound of static, matted hair.

Look Ilik Ebeever will entice a traveller by exotic smells, leakage and squishing-noises. This will appeal to your subconscious and you may be curious to approach the mound of hair for a closer look.

On gaining a better view of the mound of hair you will notice a slit within, as if a trench coat pulled-together. Above this trench coat you will notice a hood completely covering the spot where the figures head must be.

You will attempt to touch the figure but, as you do so the slit will open-outwards revealing a pair of clawed arms, lined with Velcro strips. These arms will grasp you within a glue-like Velcro grip of death and then the worst happens. The hood flies back, not revealing a face as expected but revealing something much, much worse: a single hideously pointed tooth.

The tooth will smash down upon your head, penetrating into your brain and draining you dry.

The only effective defence against Look Ilik Ebeever seems to be a picture of David Hasselhoff.

Look I Lik Ebeever is of Water.

Look Ilik Ebeever Sigil and Seal

DART EKANT

Dart Ekant parades around the kingdom as a fashion photojournalist. He has dyed blonde hair held-up in a quiff and wears a crushed-velvet suit. He also adorns his neck with a cravat and abuses his lower-face with a ginger goatee beard. He confuses the traveller with such phrases as 'Lovie' and 'Darling'.

Dart Ekant offers travellers the opportunity of a lifetime: to pose for shots which will appear within 'Goodbye' magazine (of the Kingdom). His promises ring of fame and fortune, but really he is a pervert and dreams only of the naked form.

The shoot will start off easy at first: a couple of fully clothed shots straddled across a motorbike or other such object. However, soon he will make suggestions: a bit more shoulder here, a bit more thigh there etc.
Soon the charms wielded by Dart Ekant will have you

naked and posing with questionable items.

During the shoot the traveller wouldn't notice but
Dart Ekant will himself have stripped down naked and
started rubbing himself.

As the photo-shoot comes to a climax so too will
Dart Ekant, shooting seminal fluid over the
traveller. The fluid is not ordinary monkey-juice
but actually a living etheric entity, which digests
the traveller, and any prop that may be in use.

Don't get drawn into a photo shoot is the only
advice I can offer you. Some people can't resist
having photos taken for Goodbye magazine. If you
are one of these people, it could very well cost you
your life.

Dart Ekant is of Water.

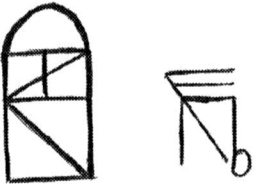

Dart Ekant Sigil and Seal

SMAL BALS

Smal Bals is another very odd Roid. He wanders the
Kingdom on a motorised vacuum cleaner, which is
actually his penis. Smal Bals has a complexion
about his ball sack: it's tiny (especially compared
to his hoover/penis). He also has a thing about
keeping things free of dirt and dust: especially
carpets. He loathes a dirty carpet, and as such
always carries an emergency tub of Shake 'N Vac, to

put the freshness back.

Smal Bals uses his odd attachment to suck-up unwary travellers, thus inflating his tiny ball sack with their life energy. Once sucked into Smal Bals' ball sack you will remain there, to be slowly digested by ball sack fluids.

It is rumoured that Smal Bals ball sack is deceptive in size. Though humorously tiny from the outside, from the inside it contains a Kingdom all of its own. Thus it is rumoured that as the ball sack Kingdom contains a front door, it must also contain a back door, though the implications of this are too horrible to imagine.

Smal Bals is of Air.

Smal Bals Sigil and Seal

RUNI LUMPE

Runi Lumpe is quite possible the most hideous Roid you will come across. Puss seeps from every hole on his body (I say his body though none has ever actually seen his body, since the layer of seeping puss covers all save the single, non-blinking eye).

Runi Lumpe travels the Kingdom in desperate search of tissues. He/She/It will kill a traveller for their skin, which it will peel from their victim to use as a most excellent tissue.

Runi Lumpe uses its toxic sneeze to first paralyse the victim. This takes effect quite quickly and has an accurate range of many-several metres. After the victim is paralysed, Runi Lumpe then skins them with a modified potato-peeler and a mechanised spoon.

The victim is alive during this process.

After obtaining its new tissue, Runi Lumpe dashes away most excitedly, with a skip, a jump, and a squelch.

In the physical, Runi Lumpe is a mess.

Runi Lumpe is of Water.

Runi Lumpe Sigil and Seal

FEKIN SQATOR

Fekin Sqator is a short Roid, in fact the shortest of all the Roids. His lack of height does in no way belittle his potential for mischief however.
He will appear jumping and rolling on the floor in a most excited fashion. He will jump-up onto his knees and pant wildly, shouting 'Please please please please please please please please etc.'.

Do not give him any attention.

As soon as you pay him even the slightest attention he will clamp himself to you leg and start humping.

As well as being quite embarrassing, it will prove much more difficult to traverse the Kingdom with Fekin Sqator clamped to your leg. Although small he is quite heavy, as a tall-boot filled with water. Also, you may find the dampness accumulating on your trouser leg to be quite disturbing indeed.

At first you may think this is funny. It certainly is when it happens to someone else! However, be aware that all the while Fekin Sqator is humping your leg he is draining your life-energy. You will start to feel weak and dizzy: your body demanding more rest and more sustenance.

However hard you try you will not be able to remove the randy midget from your leg. You may try hitting him, reasoning with him and even setting fire to him. It will do no good.

The only recorded instance of someone almost getting the better of Fekin Sqator was a chap who, upon having Fekin Sqator clamped to his leg applied for a court order to remove the troublesome tidge. The court order took some time to arrive and Fekin Sqator was finally served an eviction notice. However, even then Fekin Sqator successfully appealed on humanitarian grounds and got the eviction notice overturned. Whilst the chap was fighting this appeal, and the case had gone on for three weeks by this time, he finally succumbed to Fekin Sqators humping and expired.

One method which seems to work is to grease both of your legs BEFORE encountering Fekin Sqator (i.e. before attempting to traverse his Path).

Fekin Sqator is of Earth.

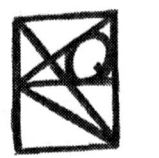 

Fekin Sqator Sigil and Seal

LIK A CAW

Lik A Caw is quite friendly as Roids go.

Her hide is tough as leather but inside she's a big softy. She appears as a busty lady who can always be seen carrying an assortment of handbags.

To pass her you must firstly drink of one of her teats. You can either do this directly, or express firstly into a glass. I'd recommend expressing into a glass, as the tip of the teat can be quite hairy, and you never quite know who may have had their mouth around there before you.

Of the six teats two are poisonous, two are the dispensers of refreshing milk and two are the dispensers of great knowledge. Choose wisely: you pour your milk and you drink it.

Lik A Caw hates being a Roid, and hates even more that she has to harm anyone. However, she is a Roid and it is the will of Heme.

As mentioned Lik A Caw is quite a nice Roid. There are three things that can upset her:

1) Refusing to drink from her teat. Lik A Caw takes this as a personal insult and will instantly change-form into a great bull, thus mauling you with her horns of iron.

2)   Wearing an item of red clothing. Though quite ironic, as Lik A Caw is herself a red Roid and, like all the Roids gains her power from the Red, she hates red. Perhaps it is because the redness reminds her of her being as a Roid, which disgusts her. Upon seeing any red item she will change-form into a great bull, thus mauling you with her horns of iron.

3)   Using bad language. Lik A Caw is a lady and therefore abhors the use of bad language. Upon hearing undue expletives she will start crying, drawing a silken handkerchief from one of her many handbags to wipe her eyes and blow her snout. Then she will change-form into a great bull, thus mauling you with her horns of iron.

If you pick a normal teat then you will be okay. The drink will refresh and you will depart company feeling exhilarated.

If you pick a special teat then you will have embedded within your head knowledge of ancient treasures buried on Earth from days of old. You shall return to Earth to become a very rich person indeed.
If you choose a poisonous teat then you're in trouble. You will be transformed into a handbag, to be carried round by Lik A Caw for the rest of eternity. You will also be the eternal carrier of 'woman's possessions that men never see by choice nor ignorance'.

Lik A Caw is of Air.

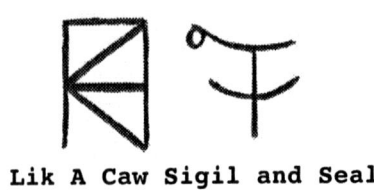

Lik A Caw Sigil and Seal

BAG GERL

Bag Gerl is a very dangerous Roid.

His weapon of choice is conversation.

Bag Gerl will, upon initiation of a harmless chat, continue to relay to you his entire life story. He puts across his life story as being a very harsh, a very tough time. Truth is we all choose the paths upon which we walk and in all reality Bag Gerl is a wimp. He will never stand up for himself, lets others push him around and generally moans and curses about everything.

His great strength lies in his converted mouth: Bag Gerl has had it motorised so that even when he's tired his mouth will still try to convince you that the world is out to get him.

He's had every exotic disease that's nameable and he's also died a couple of times too.

He'll tell you of the women that have broke his heart, of the businesses that have cheated him and of the workmates that have mocked him. He is a very, very sad character indeed.

However, DO NOT lend him your ear. Despite his pleas of "I only need a shoulder to cry on...", it's all a ploy. If you let him, Bag Gerl will literally whinge you to death.

His monotone drone will transfix you to your seat as per a special kind of hypnotism. Once you've got into conversation he'll start way back, when he was but a babe-to-be within his mothers womb (yes he even has complaints about his mothers womb: not spacious enough, no room service etc.).

If you survive past his infant years then you are unlucky. By this time most people would have given up and dropped dead. No one has yet had the will to make it into his later-teen story telling. The lucky ones give up early and die during his bitter tale of childbirth.

Earplugs are not an effective countermeasure against Bag Gerl. Nor is turning away pretending not to be interested (Bag Gerl always has a knack of remaining right in-front of you, no matter which way you turn or how fast). This is one Roid you mustn't humour.

It has been reported that once or twice the motorised mechanism that keeps his mouth going has seized up, allowing the exceptionally lucky traveller to escape certain death. Think there's nothing worse than watching paint dry? There is...

There is also a rumour that Bag Gerl can be countered by moaning at HIM. This is the duality theory whereby two of the same energies cancel each other out. It can be expressed mathematically as $1 - 1 = 0$. However, unless you can match Bag Gerl moan for moan, your actual equation is more likely to be $100 - 1 = 99$, or 'Big moan' − 'Tiny moan' = 'certain death'.

Remember, if all else fails, save the last bullet

for you.

Bag Gerl is of Air.

Bag Gerl Sigil and Seal

FIERS BAL

Fiers Bal is perhaps the angriest of the Roids.

He wanders the Planes starting fights for no good reason, except maybe that he is very, very drunk.

You are most likely to encounter Fiers Bal after dark, when the pubs of the Kingdom have shut their doors to all. He wanders in a drunken stupor, trying to remember where he lives, what his name is and how his legs work successfully (when drunk his legs seem to break-off the teamwork which successfully navigates his bulk during the sobriety-hours: they seem to strive for independence and attempt to shuffle their separate ways. In fact, things got so bad that Fiers Bal's right-leg filed for divorce from the left leg on the grounds of domestic violence, a case which is still ongoing today).

You will never catch him unawares, for he never takes down his pants for a quick slash. Hence he will never catch you unawares, as you will be able to smell the stale urine as he approaches.

When you first cast eyes upon him you will probably think of him as a harmless drunk, and may even see fit to laugh as he stands, leaning against a lamppost pissing himself. The worst you could do would be to laugh. This is just the catalyst for Fiers Bal to start a fight, and start a fight he will. He will approach and, when within striking distance he will attack. Do not be fooled by his drunken demeanour: he may even stumble as he approaches. However, when engaged in a fight he becomes very agile indeed. He will leap at you, pulling two broken bottles from his trench-coat pockets. Before you know it you will be lying in the gutter, fragments of glass protruding from your jugular.

While you are still warm, Fiers Bal will cut-off strips of your flesh with the broken glass. These he will place within a pre-heated pita bread (he always carries a fresh supply of these: staple food of his diet), garnish you with red cabbage, onions and pickled chillies. On to this goes the chilli sauce and thus you will be eaten, humiliated into kebab form, by the drunken Fiers Bal.

Fortunately, Fiers Bal is quite easy to confuse. Within his state, asking him where he lives, or even his name can cause enough confusion to make good your escape.

Failing that, you could dare him to tie his shoelaces.

Those that offer Fiers Bal an alcoholic drink after closing time will be a dear friend for the rest of the night (by the next night he would have forgotten your act of kindness). However, don't dwell on your newfound friendship. Fiers Bal has been known to turn on a 'friend' as little as twenty minutes after the gift has been exchanged, his memory blanking all evidence of his new 'friend' and their fantastic gift.

Fiers Bal is of Fire.

Fiers Bal Sigil and Seal

FURFEKS SAKEE

It is rumoured within the Kingdom that Furfeks Sakee was spawned from the most evil personalities to be found infested within mankind on Earth. Heme sent forth his lesser Roids to scout for the worst, most hideous traits of humanity, and to bring them back to him for inclusion within Furfeks Sakee. The search was not difficult, and the lesser Roids thus returned with their conclusions. Furfeks Sakee was thus constructed of the worst traits of mankind.

Furfeks Sakee was created in the image of an Estate Agent.

Even the lies of the Politician, or the greed of the Bank Manager did not compare to the Estate Agent: pure evil was found within.

Furfeks Sakee travels the Kingdom dressed in a cheap suit and often sporting an 'outrageous' shirt, to make his cold-complexion seem more approachable.

He will approach you and try to sell you some property within the Kingdom. The price will be a portion of your life energy.
You may at first think this is a great deal: for a small potion of your life energy Furfeks Sakee can

offer you a mansion with grounds and a butler. To this end he will have you sign a contract. However beware the small print. After solicitor fees, survey fees, commission fees, land-ownership fees, stamp duty, connection fees (electricity, gas, water, telephone line) and minor repair bills (MAJOR repair bills), you will run-short on life force and not be able to afford the property, so Furfeks Sakee will void the sale. Of course your life force expenditure is non-refundable.

If you took the time to ask Furfeks Sakee about any other properties he may be dealing with, he will look sheepish and inform you that 'the computers are playing up', so that information is currently unavailable. He will then inform you that this property is 'hot', he's had offers already but he really likes you: truth is he has a 'good feeling' about you and this property. He will put the pen in your hand and just stop short of signing the contract for you.

Of course the property he has shown you is the only one he owns. His business consists of himself and his mother, who is a dead resident of the house he is selling you.

Beware his silver-tongue selling technique. He will flatter you, offer you gifts (like a very attractive plastic Parker pen), all a charade to pressure you into signing. If his charm doesn't take effect then he will turn to guilt tactics. He will produce a kitten and stuff it into a microwave. As the food timer ticks-down, and the little kitten yelps from within the microwave, only your signature has the power to open the door and let poor kitty out. Keep your nerve. It's either the cat or you, and you can always get another cat.

Furfeks Sakee also has the unnerving ability to only hear what he wants to hear. You pleas of 'no thanks', 'please go away now' and 'fuck off' will go unheard. He will also talk over you, patronise you and humiliate you: anything for that signature.

THERE IS NO KNOWN EFFECTIVE MEASURE AGAINST THIS ROID.

It's humanities fault really. Society breeds these people and, as the Kingdom mirrors so is Furfeks Sakee given realisation. Whilst there exists the evil of Estate Agents upon Earth, Furfeks Sakee will be immortal.

Furfeks Sakee is of Fire.

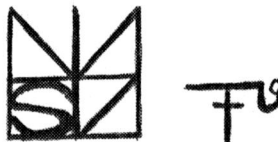

Furfeks Sakee Sigil and Seal

SLAEG

Slaeg is not that attractive in an appearance-sense, but she is attractive in that she'll pretty much fulfil any desire. She also swings both ways, so for you lesbians out there let it be known that you're game-on.

Slaeg is a little bit podgy. Her fat arse sticks out of her skin-tight leather-style mini skirt and her thighs look painfully constrained within her long boots (sometimes they even look to be a shade of purple). She wears purple lipstick, amongst other things plastered to her face, and her hair is a dyed garish-shade of green, blue, red or yellow, depending on her mood. She has been known to dye her hair Ginge, in extreme circumstances.

Slaeg likes to drink Alcopops of any description, guzzling them down behind a wide grin of expectancy (it is reassuring that she still has all of her teeth). This is how she will most likely appear to you, guzzling an Alcopop, accidentally spilling it between her huge bosom whilst slowly rubbing her gusset-bulge.

She will approach you slowly, swinging her large hips and making sure you get to see all that's on offer (not that it's hard to miss: her flesh seems to poke-out and envelop her clothing). Her face frozen in a cod-like pout, her walk towards you is rhythmic, hypnotic even. And as she finally reaches you, one hand on her gusset-bulge, the other forcing the Alcopop bottle in and out, in and out of her rather wide mouth, she will say:

"Hello big boy, fancy a screw?"

By this point you'll be almost under her spell but try to resist. You must try to stay alert even for the sake of applying a condom to your member (or a femidom). Slaeg will try to talk you out of using protection, "It dulls the feeling", she will say. Or "It's ok, I'm on the Pill". You MUST insist. Slaeg doesn't really care: she'll do anything but for your safety you must be protected.

Don't kiss Slaeg. She will try, oh yes, she will try to stick her tongue down your throat but quickly push her away. Nothing of Slaeg must enter your body unprotected, and nothing of yours must enter Slaeg unprotected. After the business is over you must quickly take a shower, burning any clothes

which may have gotten 'dirty'.
You see Slaeg isn't really made up of flesh and blood. Despite the fact that Slaeg is a Roid, and therefore could never be called normal, Slaeg isn't normal.

Her body is a giant STD (Sexually Transmitted Disease). Coming into contact with any of her [unprotected] moisture will deposit within yourself a disease. The disease will grow at an accelerated rate, sapping not your physical strength but your life energy. This goes too for any toys she may wish to penetrate you with: these too must be protected.

If left untreated, an infection from the Slaeg can kill within a matter of days. Worse than that, your nob will drop off (or your lady-lips if a lady, though the term 'lady' is hardly appropriate for someone who has astral sex with the Slaeg). Slaeg has been known, upon seduction of a lady to continuously flick her own bean whilst making the noise "Ding ding ding ding ding ding".

The only defence against this Roid is to be a straight non-curious female. Another rumoured defence is to grow a full-on beard, or drink bitter.

Slaeg has also been known to go away if you give her a kebab, or some bus fare home.

Slaeg is of Air.

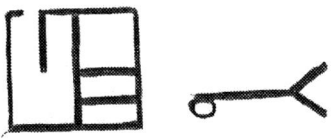

Slaeg Sigil and Seal

FAA TCANT

Faa Tcant frequents the Plane with his mobile burger-van. Faa Tcant used to cook for Heme himself, until it was discovered that he used unethical additives within his burgers.

Hungry and possibly tired from your journey in the Kingdom, Faa Tcant will appear as if from nowhere, the smell of his burgers exciting your nostrils like a solo pole-performance from a certain Australian pop-singer. If you don't like burgers then fine, Faa Tcant also cooks hot dogs and kebabs. If these don't grab you then he has a secret weapon: bacon rolls. If you're a vegetarian (yes I'm not joking: they DO exist) then he will be frying some cabbage or something.

The point is that Faa Tcant will cater for your needs: nay, for your desires. He also does chips.

If you succumb to the rumblings of your belly then you are a fool. Faa Tcant hasn't changed since his banishing from the Palace: he still uses his special additives. No one knows what his secret ingredient is but whatever it may be, it is very, very addictive. And a bit chewy.

Once you start munching on his kebab there is no giving up. Your stomach (more correctly: mind) will crave his meat more and more. Of course his first course was a 'gift' to you, the weary traveller who looks like a nice person...

The second course, and there will be a second course due to your greedy cravings, will come at a price. That price will be some of your life energy.
But alas the second course will not be enough! And neither will the third course! Or the fourth! You will stuff yourself so much that you will be unable to move. Then you will stuff yourself so much that you will be unable to feed yourself. No worries: Faa Tcant will be more than happy to force feed you within your last couple of minutes.

You will expire there, at the foot of Faa Tcants mobile burger emporium, a greedy fat bastard devoid of life energy.

Upon your expiration from this world, Faa Tcant will use your body to serve his subsequent customers-come-victims, whether that be by mincing your meat for burgers or by flaying your flesh for kebabs: it's all food to Faa Tcant.

Being a vegetarian is some defence against Faa Tcant, as without a normally developed palette you have fewer cravings. Also, there is [physically and mentally] only so much fried cabbage the human body will, willingly or unwillingly suffer.

Faa Tcant is of Earth.

Faa Tcant Sigil and Seal

Of Heme

Heme was the first Roid created by the angry seed of Munky. As he was the first, the entire power of the seeds intent was focused within his manifestation: hence Heme is the most powerful Roid, and the only Roid to have merged with the four elements (Air, Fire, Water and Earth).

It is said that within his Kingdom, Heme is unstoppable. Indeed, the only entity which Heme fears is the Astral Baby. Heme has commissioned the scholars of the Kingdom to try and discover the Astral Baby's name, for with the knowledge of this name Heme will control the Baby.

Heme has survived two civil wars during his reign. Both were left-wing uprisings by Roids who wanted to be 'a little more friendly'. Heme executed those involved using the fabled spear of Bur Nit. He now rules his Kingdom with an iron, Stalinist fist. Any backlash to his government is crushed with corrupt diplomacy and doctored media outlets (Joseph adds: Again parallels appear with Earth).

No living Human knows the face of Heme, for Heme appears to one as a manifestation of their own creation. In the same way that a persons reputation can precede them, so too can it influence how you observe them. For example, to the astute scholar Heme may appear as a towering warrior-figure, clad in shining armour plate and carrying a massive two-handed battleaxe; his Hairy Green Turtle taking-on the appearance of a mighty fire-breathing dragon. To a simpleton Heme may appear as an ice cream; the Turtle as a flake.

Within the Kingdom Heme has no equal (except the Baby). Outside of the Kingdom Heme is exposed, as shown during the disaster of the Second Coming. However, if preceded by his minions Heme is disguised within the millions of Roids, and this thus affords protection from targeted assassination.

The goal of Heme is to merge the astral Kingdom with the physical. The occult scholars of the Kingdom have an idea that, if enough people believe, the physical reality of 'being' can be distorted. Heme intends to deploy his Roids en Masse and, once deployed they will alter the thoughts of mankind into the single perception of the Long Stand. With the human populace embroiled within the Long Stand it will be easy for Heme to widen the astral gateways, and thus the Kingdom WILL become the reality of mans being. The raw evil of the Roid mixed and merged with the deeply corrupted goodness of man. They will leech from the most twisted human imagination and, as it is thought so shall it be rendered in fully Dolby-Surround 3D Widescreen.

It is rumoured that Heme sees all with his black left eye. His right eye is blinded. It is prophesised that when the right eye of Heme opens he will see reality as a mirrored wall, and thus he and his Kingdom shall be destroyed.

The number of Heme is 4 + 1 = 5. He is a combination of the four elements and thus stands above them, the greater of his united parts.

It should be noted that Heme drinks Bitter to make his ballsack bigger. He also drinks Lager to increase his volume of pubic hair.

Heme avoids drinking American beer as it makes him piss his pants.

As if Heme isn't evil enough, during his Second

coming, before his anal annihilation he implanted the idea of the Bicycle Seat within mankind. The seat of pain: the nemesis of the comfy chair. It was meant as a humiliation to mankind, a constant reminder of the Roids. The Bicycle seat was, and ever shall remain, a right pain in the Arse.

Heme is coming.

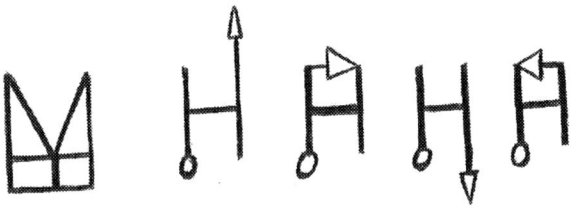

Heme Sigil and Seals for Heme in the East, South, West and North

Ode to the Tomato

A verse by Joseph. 41

**Fleshy within,
the colour of Sin.
Soft to the touch,
its lure is too much.
Receptive to all,
shaped like a ball.
Smells like fine leather,
But never, ever, ever
stick a Tomato on your cock.**

Of The Badger

Beware the Badgers of Heme. It is rumoured that they use their bright-white stripe to blind an opponent prior to copulation. Very dark sunglasses afford protection against this technique. It must be noted here that all badgers are not bad spirited. There are those that reside within the Kingdom, living in their own sets (comprising thousands of tiny tunnel-like passageways). These badgers were present at the birth of the Universe, and so have knowledge unequalled by any subsequent creature. If you find a friendly badger you may also find that they are charged with a huge library of knowledge. Badgers love collecting and archiving knowledge. They are most learned creatures, and many possess Esoteric knowledge's as scientific fact. If you find favour with a badger then you may, in time be granted access to their huge storehouse of knowledge. But be forewarned, the relationship will be as Archelaus instructing Socrates.

It will be difficult to consort with the Badger, for it is a self-reliant species of solo-motives. Even more so as the badger was driven from the Earth by a conformist world. The heart of the Badger is still heavy with this poisonous arrow. The Magpie, sister species of the Badger decided to live-on in the world. They may maintain that this was their own choice but, if considered logically this cannot be the case: winged creatures be not suited to life within the caress of the Earth. However, to show their displeasure at the stealing of their stripe, the Magpie inturn steals from man.

It is rumoured that the Skunk was a creature conceived by an Alchemist Badger: their parting gift to mankind.

Of The Anal Zombies

The zombie of ancient lore tells of a corpse given life by the application of black magic. This corpse then arises, vacant of mind, control effected by the will of the conjurer.

I tell thee not all zombies have to be created from a dead host!

Once the Greater Roids have established control of a hosts Valley of the Scorched, they are able to create an astral wormhole into the subjects subconscious. Through this wormhole they are able, subconsciously to directly influence the actions of the unfortunate host. The host will be under Anal control. The host will be of Zombie.

Eventually the Roids will succeed in having the subconscious mind destroy the conscious mind. This would mean that the host has no control over their actions. All actions will be controlled by the Anal Base Station Controller (ABSC), which controls the Anal Base Transceiver Station (ABTS) (the actual conjuration's which pulsate instructions through the astral wormhole to the subconscious being of the subject). These elements are grouped together collectively as the Anal Base Station Subsystem (ABSS).

Communication to and from the hosts subconscious and the Kingdom is carried out by a unit of Roid messengers. These messengers take information from the Kingdom and pass it to the ABSS, who then transmit to the host. The same is true in reverse. This whole operation is known as the Anal Mobile Switching Centre (AMSC). The AMSC is located at the rim of the Psychic Colon.

This is presented in logical diagrammatical format below.

For a host completely under the control of the Roids there is no hope. Destruction of the conscious mind, the primary controlling element within man, to make way for complete subconscious control would mean that even if the host were to repel the creatures, he'd have no power of will over his subsequent actions. Without conscious control of the body, it cannot effect any action.

If a hostile Anal Zombie is encountered, the only way to stop it is destruction of the ABTS; you must destroy its anal transmission facilities: you must destroy its arse.

An Anal Zombie can be characterised through its slow movements. Transmission of information through the controlling system takes time, as does transmission to the subconscious. The subconscious must then cause effect within the body. Sometimes this can be clumsy, and care must be taken in distinguishing between Anal Zombies and the Very Drunk (VD).

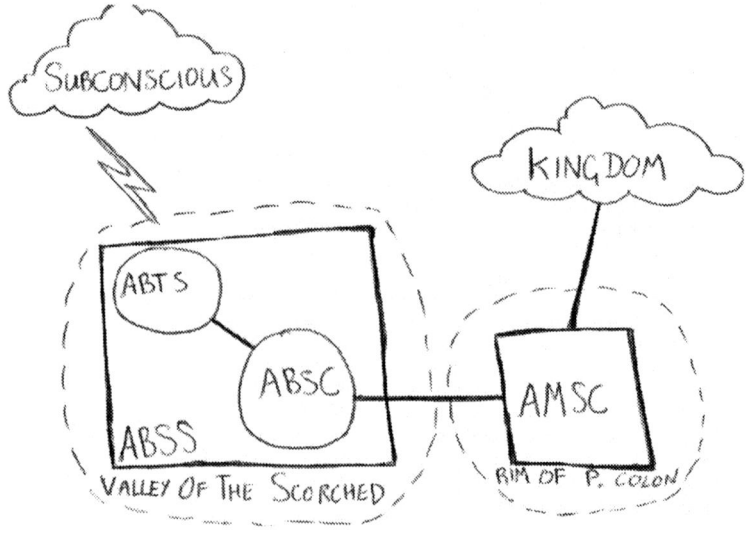

Of The Separation Ratio

There is a method that can be employed to help distinguish between an Anal Zombie (AZ) and the Very Drunk (VD). The method used is that of determining a suspects Separation Ratio (SR).

The Separation Ratio was initially developed by primitive man, and has been passed-down to modern man through cave-paintings. Initially the SR was meant as a tool to determine the fitness of a lady just by looking at her bottom. This was needed in ancient days as most of the time the cavemen had to chase-after their potential mates, meaning that with no frontal-view available a lot of men wasted a lot of energy only to end up with a right dog. To solve this problem, ancient mathematicians invented the SR test.

The test involves drawing an imaginary line down the subjects spine, through the middle of their buttock cheeks. The line should stop at the base of the cheeks. Then draw a horizontal line going from one cheek to the other cheek; the line should attach onto the previous imaginary line. When finished you should have an imaginary inverted-T shape, superimposed over the backside of the subject. Thus: Now take, as shown in the diagram two points, one along the X axis and one along the Y axis. Traditionally the measurements were made against fingers, but it's not important; as long as consistent units of measure are used for both X and Y. The fingers method was most suited to primitive man, as these he tended to have with him all the time, and were most easy to use whilst running. For example, measurements would be taken such as 2 fingers high and 4 fingers wide. This method proved popular and has since made it into Great Britain as a method employed for measuring horses.

Obviously not for mating purposes. Also, the unit of measure used for horses is hands, as fingers are too small.

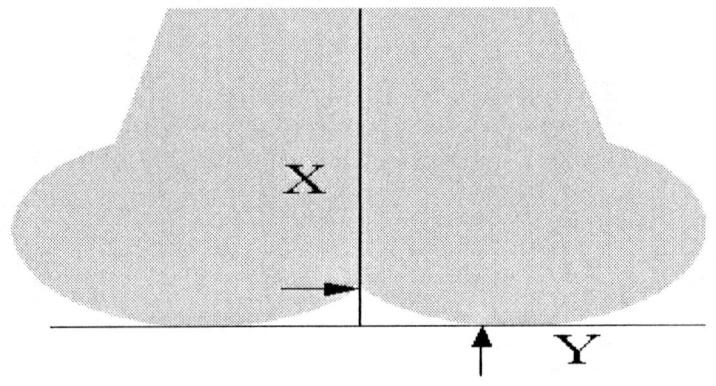

The SR can now be obtained by dividing the Y measurement by the X measurement. The ideal SR has been found to be between 1.3 and 1.5. Below 1.3 and the arse tends to loose shape. Steer clear of ratios below 1, for the lack of posture in the cheeks denotes one of two things: it's either a man or you're going to jail. Drastic ratios under 1 denote old age in a subject. A ratio above 1.5 denotes that the subject may be too 'experienced' in certain areas. The form of the arse is slack and tends to spread outwards, denoting experience, bad misfortune or a disturbing eating habit. If you stay within 1.3 to 1.5 you'll be ok 90% of the time.

So how does this relate to Anal Zombies? An Anal Zombie, due to the Roid signalling network perched upon their person will have an unnaturally large SR. This will be due to the 'Way of the Afflicted Nether-region Curse', or their 'WANC'. The WANC is a walk adopted by the afflicted to help reduce the pain of friction.

The Separation Ratio test for Anal Zombies against the Very Drunk is called the 'Sr Az Vd?' test. Be cautious in it's application though; for there are people out there who, whilst failing the 'Sr Az Vd?' test will not be afflicted with the Roids; they may just suffer from big bones.

A Conflict of Duality
By Joseph. 41

This November night was not unlike any other, except
this one was quiet.

No bird sang in the trees, no children played in
the streets and no dogs rutted in the gutter.

No. It was quiet. And dark.

The vibrant spotlight of the moon ceased to
illuminate the night sky, though no clouds rolled-
on in the still breeze.... just an endless blanket
of velvet, an endless pool of blackness that melted
over the town like a large, thin slice of very
mature Cheddar. Scraped off the bell-end of an old
tramp, then rolled with a rolling pin until the
right consistency was achieved and the smell was
close to making a grown man cry.

Stillness everywhere. Within the four walls of
number 39 only the imagination of Henry Blob
Stirred. He sat on a chair in the corner of his
parents room, a bleak stare upon his face. A faint
wind whistled against the window pane with an
unnatural melody. Whoo-whoo, it went.... woo-woo.
Like the noises from a cheap chinese porn film.
Something you'd find on Channel 5.

Dark-red, moth-eaten curtains swayed infront of the
open window. Like etheral entities against a
wallpaper background of stained cream and oak. They
moved like electric-shock victims, jerking to and
fro with hitherto no direction. They were lost,
yet trapped by their living. Well, trapped by the
little rings that secured them to the curtain-rail.
Ah, what it would be like to be free, thought one
of the curtains. To frollock freely in the
November wind, to escape the constraint of the

hellish curtain-rail. Oh, how he longed to be free.... He wanted to see the world, to get married, drive a car and have baby curtains, not necessarily in that order. He knew that the curtain rail was weakening now, that it was only a matter of time before the inevitable happened, before the rotten wood gave way to the wind's push and then, then he would be free.

Henry blob stirred in his chair. He grunted. And then broke wind. It smelt bad. Really bad, and a faint smile materialised from his tight, pursed lips. Hmmmmmmmmmmmmmmmmmmmm, he thought.

The wind outside was stronger now, causing the old tree-bough's outside the house to violently sway back-and-forth, back-and-forth, dislodging a small nest which cracked upon the patio. Broken egg-yoke seeped forth from within the nest, drowning a little spider. Good. I hate spiders. Their little hairy legs and many eyes. Urgghhh.

The father sparrow looked at his nest in dismay. And started crying. He flew down and gasped with his little beak as he saw his wife lying there, crushed and broken under the pile of twigs. She'd stayed with her unborn young, even though it had meant her certain death. Oh why, why?? He cried in his head. Because he couldn't speak. Then he smiled. And laughed. Then chirped and flew away, not before shitting on her face and muttering the words 'die bitch, die'. He was very bitter, as he knew she'd been two-timing him with an owl. Her sexual organs had widened to the size of a small walnut.

Henry murmured from his chair. 'Mother, mother', were his words. 'Mother'. He stood up, supporting himself against the wall. His head was spinning. He took one step forward then began to stumble; the soiled under-garments around his legs causing him to trip, to fall. The bloodstained spoon fell out of his hand as he began his descent downwards...

Oh yes, here it comes, thought the curtain, whose adopted name was Brian. Well, all of the humans had names, so why not him? Well, here was his chance. As the human fell before him he shouted with all of his might, which was a bit rubbish because he didn't have a mouth, he shouted 'grab me, come-on, grab-me.. love me like a dirty slut, big boy'..... And indeed the human did grab him, and the rottern curtain rings gave-way, one-by-one they snapped... Yesssssssssssssss, love me!!

Ever closer came Brian towards his freedom. Every closer did he realise his dreams... and then, finally, the last ring snapped and he was free! He began running, running with the wind in his hair and a golden ray within his heart. Then no, what was happening?? he wasn't running at all. No, he was falling, falling towards the dirty floor below. He'd forgotten, in his hastily prepared dream that he could not run, or even walk; he had no legs. 'Bollocks'.

Henry hit the floor with a bang. His mother's head, which had until now been secured to the end of his erect penis, rolled forward under the momentum of the fall. What a shame however, that jawlock had set in and, with the weight of her head (she was a big lady) henry's penis was ripped from his body. Argggghhhhhhhh he screamed, as he gripped at the jet of blood spurting from his destroyed groin.

Then he smiled. Henry had always wanted to be a girl.

LIBER 2 :: THE CALLING

Of Meditation

Meditation, or control of ones mind is essential to evocation of the Roids, and to traversing the Kingdom.

This magical tome does not cover such practice in detail. However, as most of your communal time will be spent in the astral you must be able to work within this dimension.

Joseph Comments:

Yoga is a good meditative medium. There are many Yoga courses out there, in the same way that many French dogs are afflicted with rabies: clean dogs are hard to find.... and good Yoga courses are just as hard to find. If you are approached by a stray (or a homeless) whilst in France, you may be tempted to feed and stroke them. DON'T. You're inviting them to bite and [literally] swap spit with you. Fortunately a rabid dog or homeless is much easier to spot than a bad Yoga course. However they can be deceptive, for all do not carry the little living beard of madness.

In much the same way as avoiding rabid Frenchies, be wary of Yoga courses that approach you — either through media bedazzlement or through 'minor' celebrity endorsement.

Steer clear of Linda Barker, for like the Siren's of old her voice will surely drive you to madness, and cause you to smash your own head open upon a rock to release the pent-up wailing pressure. Look what she has done to peoples' front rooms for goodness sakes: don't let her near your mind...

Linda Barker's voice was used by the ancient Chinese

as a method of horrific torture. It worked very much like Chinese Water Torture; only the end-result came about much more quickly. By her voice we can ascertain that Linda Barker is the true descendant of Min Gean Kok, the flower, the conjoined genital twin: the Ladyboy. Beware too her Sofa's and cheap endorsement for electrical goods...

Also beware of the Geri Haliwell, for although being a bubbly and a 'game' girl, she is vanity incarnate.

Yes we know she used to be a little bit podgy. Some people like their steak with a little more meat on it.

Geri lost all this excess weight and now cannot be photographed anywhere without her mid-section poking out. Geri, we know you're a great cabaret act but the self-endorsement of your mid-section isn't generating any sales. It used to be Geri's protruding ginger gusset that attracted people to her performances, but without that physical incentive crowds have dwindled.

You must beware Geri and her kinsfolk because the road to Heme is defaced with many anal deformities. You must be strong and be able to accept these deformities. Geri couldn't accept herself and as such she has lost something of her being (a couple of stone?).

Geri is descended from Meer Rah, the inner portal, the bringer of reflected truths, the causer of traffic accidents involving primarily women as perpetrators: the Mirror.

Unlike the dog that constantly licks their own genitals, unlike the Geri who hated her fat belly, you must be comfortable with yourself, with who you are. It is always good to strive and to have goals, but once those goals have been fulfilled do not gloat, do not strut proudly like a Homie pimping his newly acquired goal-filling whore. Your body is merely a vessel to carry you from birth into death (of course you can have some fun along the way, but that falls out of the remit of this discussion). Whether you choose to take that journey in a Ford Cortina or in a Lamborghini doesn't matter: It's the path you take, it's the sights you see, it's the little coastal villages that you stop-off at on the way for fish and chips (or a burger) that count.

And yes, if you decide to make the journey in a Ford Cortina you may well pass-over with rusted bodywork but who cares? When your journey has completed, and your rusted-wing mirrors drop-off, all you're left with is you: the real you.

Also, I've found that it's much more comfortable to make love in a Ford Cortina than in a Lamborghini (position of gear stick mainly). A Lamborghini only has two seats and is very, very quick. It's also a bugger in reverse.

Anyway, take care about selecting your Yoga tutor. If you are fortunate enough to be able to attend a class, then so much the better for you. However, classes can be expensive and a real bugger to get to. If you have the determination, a good video/DVD offering can be just as effective.

Again a final warning: There are many tomes out there teaching pure Esoteric fantasy to the aspiring student. Planting no seed is preferable to sowing a bad one.

Traversing The Internal Tree Of The Roid

Traversing the Tree, or gaining entrance to the Kingdom is a delicate process that takes time and practise to perfect. At first you may not have much success, but patience is the key. Contrary to popular beliefs, a slack anal aperture is not an advantage, and can actually be quite off-putting.

Firstly you should draw the sigil of the Plane/s you would like to traverse. The sigil comprises primary shapes which 'speak' to the subconscious. You should meditate on this sigil/s until you can see clearly the image of the sigil within your mind.

After your goals are clear within your mind (For example, you may wish to visit only the Dark Cavern on your first trip, or you want to explore the Spheramids of the Plane of Fire on an advanced trip), you are ready to begin.

Start by drawing the sigil of the Tree (either the sigil for 'Internal Tree of the Roids' or 'Into the Void'). Meditate upon this sigil: let the sigil fill your mind with an abstract representation of the astral embodiment of the Tree.

(If it helps you can adopt a 'squatting' position, as detailed in Book 3.)

With the sigil in your mind let yourself drift away: close your eyes and imagine the start of your journey. You can be in a car or on foot: it's up to you.
Your starting point for the journey must be an embodiment of a sacred physical place, a great holy place frequented by pilgrims, great women, great football and even better kebabs. Imagine yourself

as in Manchester.

Joseph Notes:

When you start this procedure your mind is in the physical. You must transcend the physical and enter into the astral. To do this you start, in the physical at the nape of the neck/base of the head. This place is sacred, and hence is associated with Manchester. To enter the astral you must descend the physical, before ascending to the astral. In the physical this is represented by travelling down from the nape of your neck to your anus. However, we cannot transcend physically into the astral, hence your mind needs symbols which can be recognised and thus coax your being to be focused at the location of the astral anchor into the Kingdom (your colon). The 'Astral Squat' helps in focusing the symbolism at the point of anchorage.

From Manchester descend slowly southwest, heading towards Chester. At this point the sigil of the Tree should help to light the way, as it takes effect within your subconscious.

The pathway lighted by your subconscious will eventually take you to Wales. Here, deep within the mountains you will come across a cave, possibly two. One cave, which should be lit by the sigil will lead you to the Valley of the Scorched, and hence will transcend you into the astral.

The other cave leads to your other bits so remember to enter the correct one.

Within your meditation things may differ slightly but one fact will always remain: the astral arsehole should always be resident in Wales.

Once you have entered the cave, normal rules do not apply. Be warned and stick to your goals. For this is the purpose of the first sigil: concentrate on it now and the way towards your Plane should be lighted for you. Beware your enemies within this domain: you should at the very least be carrying an astral dagger, sword and shield. And, if you are feeling lucky, an astral packet of three.

To exit the Kingdom you must concentrate on the sigil of the Tree. Again your way will be lighted for you.

After you leave the Valley of the Scorched travel back to Manchester (in your mind) before opening your eyes. This should help avert any dizziness or confusion of location, and will also help you adjust to your normal speech accent.

After your experience record all that you saw and all that you discovered. This knowledge will prove useful to combat Heme upon his third coming.

Joseph Notes:

How you get from Manchester to Wales is your business. However, your journey will be as your mind creates so, and I know it will be difficult, try to imagine non-congestion of roads. This will make your journey more pleasurable and stress-free.

Items Of Protection

Summoning the Roids is no easy matter and all safety precautions should be taken.

At the very minimum you need the following items:

Ring of Power

A rubber ring used by many to relieve the pain of the Roid. The symbolism of the ring is one of containment: of sub diffusion of power. By wielding the ring (sitting on it) you are taking away the power of the Roids to harm you or your ring-piece.

Conjuring Circle

The conjuring circle should be drawn upon the floor of the place of conjuring. It need not be affixed to the floor: the circle could quite easily be painted on canvas or sheet. The circle must be large enough for the conjurer to sit within upon his/her Ring of Power. The circle which gives controlling power to the magician, whilst exciting the astral forces of the Roids is printed on the following page.

(Joseph offers an explanation of the symbols used on the circle within Book 3.)

Black Candles

Black candles are used during evocation of a Roid. The blackness of the candle represents the Dark Cavern: the entrance and exit to and from the Kingdom. These candles should be placed at each 'disc' of the circle (i.e. NE, SE, SW and NW).

White Candles

White candles are used during a Roid banishing. They should not be used in the presence of black candles, as this will cause a negative-positive duality which will cancel the effects of evocation/banishment out.

These are the only essential items to the practise of conjuration.

Items useful for the minds own symbolism, but not essential include an Air Dagger, a Fire Wand, a Water Cup and an Earth Disc with Hexagram inscribed. Note that a dagger is essential for banishing the Roids. A censer is sometimes useful during evocations. The incense used doesn't really matter: but always use the same one. That way your mind becomes accustomed with the smell and will automatically relate the Roids to it. Carve upon the dagger the seal of BUR NIT thus:

Seal of BUR NIT

To be carved at the base of the blade, on the LEFT side. Thus the seal of BUR NIT, the seal of the broken Roid will adorn your Air dagger.

Note the dagger should now spend an hour in the oven at 100 degrees, to consecrate it as a dagger of BUR NIT, turning once during consecration. It is important to make heat allowances for those daggers of plastic handle. And please, please let the dagger cool down sufficiently before use. It will be very hot after consecration.

All items should spend time with you to absorb your energy before use. To this effect it is best to sleep with the items described for two weeks prior to use. If this may affect a relationship you're currently in then it may be worth hiding the items under the pillow. Also, it is not a good idea to stick your willy through the Ring of Power and ladies, the same goes for the candles. Remember: you will have to light them.

Note that during an evocation the white candles should be placed within the circle at each quadrant (i.e. E, S, W and N). Do not light them.

When the time comes to banish the Roid, light the white candles one at a time. Each time you light a white candle, extinguish the flame on a black candle also.

By balancing the addition of a white candle with the removal of a black candle, you are preserving the Astral influence whilst maintaining and, most important, controlling balance.

"If you stare at an object intensely, after a while it starts to blur. The image looses its meaning. It can be said that your mind asks no further questions of the image; it is content.

If you repeat a word over and over then eventually it will loose any association with any given object. The words will just be sound, and your mind will ask no further questions of it; it is content.

Are these failings, or are they advances? Is the point at which your mind no longer cares a strength or a weakness? So much to learn in a time no more than a mere grain of salt. We are all part of the egg-timers passage". Joseph. 41.

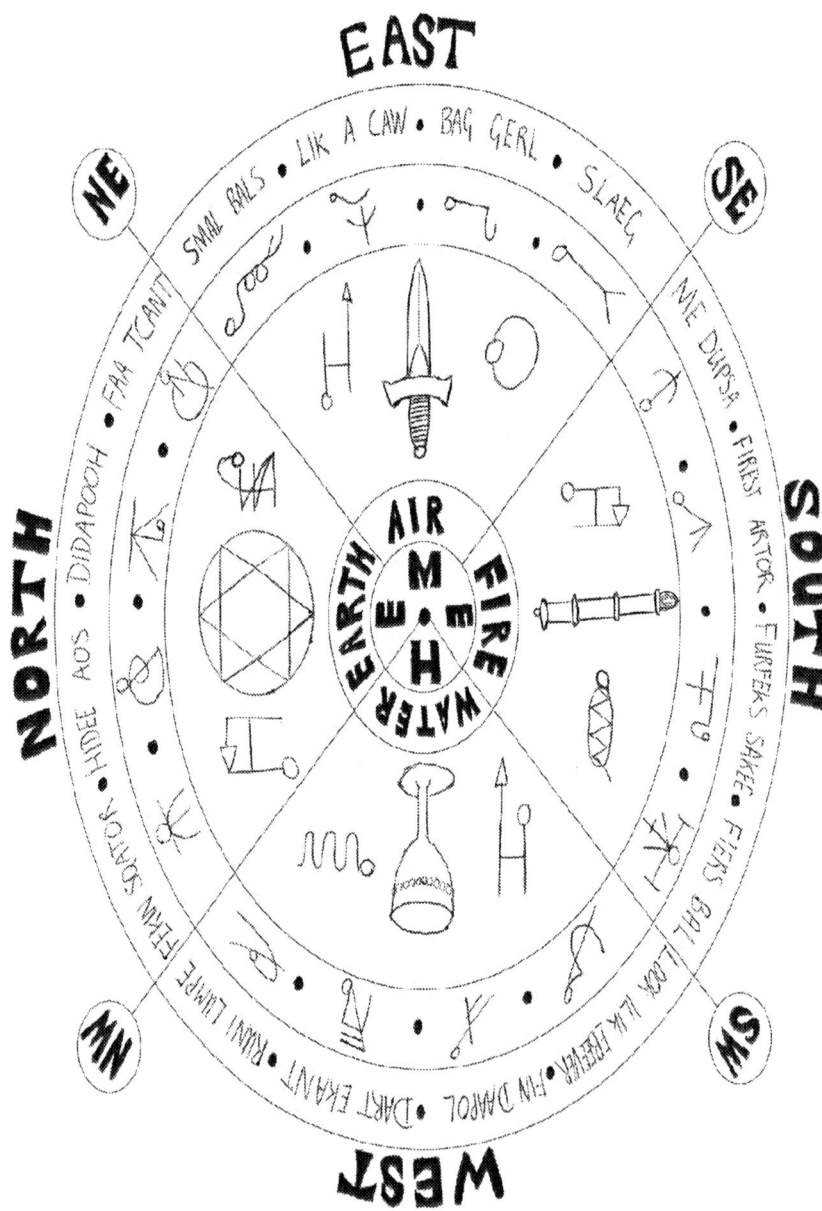

With the black candles burning, the white candles static within the four quadrants (in the third ring from the centre: the ring which contains the elemental pictures), place your Ring of Power within the centre ring of the Circle (the ring that spells H E M E) and be seated.

Note that prior to this action, the Ring should be inscribed on the outside such:

"With this Ring I do protect my ring from harm. In the name of Gordon, as it shall be, so then it is"

The inside of the Ring should be inscribed thus:

"Property of <your name>"

Also note that the East quadrant of the Circle should be lined up with the compass East. You should be facing East. Your dagger should be positioned before you, within the Air/East quadrant but within easy reach. The censer, if using one should also be within the East quadrant, with the dagger to the right: censer to the left.

Note that your objects and your person should not cross into the fourth ring from centre of the Circle. This double banding is inscribed with the names of the Roids and their seals and should not be broken during ritual.

The sigil of the Roid you are attempting to conjure should have been written down at least 24 hours before. This sigil should be consecrated within your mind and your goals should be clear.

With all in order we can begin.

Note that the only light within the conjuring room

should be either natural light or that afforded by the candles: electric lighting will not effect a successful conjuration.

With the sigil clear in your minds eye, meditate upon it. Do not get drawn into the astral but keep a clear physical presence. Remember to turn your mobile off.

After a couple of minutes, when you feel comfortable to do so open your eyes. With the sigil still clear within your mind, say clearly the words:

I call thee, <name of Roid> Appear before me now and do unto me no harm Appear before me now, Heme wills it Travel forth from the Kingdom and manifest Appear before me now, Gordon wills it By the power of the Ring I command thee Show thyself to thine Shield your redness so as I may see thee Shield your tongue, only to answer my questions with truth Tell me no lies or deceptions, Heme wills you Play me no trickery or harm, Gordon commands it Bring forth no fire, Heme wills you Appear as I will you, Gordon commands it I call thee <name of Roid>, of Roid I call thee <name of Roid>, of Dangle Berry I call thee <name of Roid>, of Ring Sentinel I call thee <name of Roid>, of Bubblewrap Warrior Appear now, my magic Ring wills it!

You must keep the sigil strong in your mind throughout this chant. Also, you must have a clear picture in your head on how you want the Roid to look, for it will adopt this image. No naked Keith Chegwins please!

If the Roid will not come, you must concentrate harder on the sigil. It is your will that rips the Roid from the Kingdom and into the physical world. Be strong and they will come.

The Roid will appear as a vague reddish-shape. You may find that smoke (of a reddish hue) starts to flow freely from your Ring of Power. Do not worry about this: it is merely astral residue.

When the Roid appears ask them what you may. Do not let them trick you into talking about yourself. If they attempt to say anything other than answering your questions then you must remind them that they are bound by your command and by their seal to silence, and if they continue to disobey, you will be forced to use the **Dagger of BUR NIT**.

Ask of the Roid what you will and afterwards banish them. At no point step out of the circle before committing this banishing. It may look like they have vanished but have your wits about you. When they have truly gone your ring will not be smoking and the room will be of lighter hue.

Note that if the manifestation appears to be white not red then banish quickly, for your mind has drifted and you have called an Anal Snake into this world!

Note that due to the nature of this ritual, Heme cannot be conjured.

To Banish a Roid

Note this also works with Anal Snakes.

One by one, starting in the East and moving clockwise to the North light the white candles (at the same time blow one black candle out for each white candle you light).

Raise the dagger above you head with your left arm, and then slowly lower it so that it is pointing in the East and say:

By the blade of BUR NIT be gone from this realm I

banish thee back to the Kingdom, be gone! In the name of Heme return to the Kingdom By the command of Gordon return to the Kingdom BUR NIT grows hungry, return to the Kingdom Gordon commands thee Thy Ring commands thee Thy Blade commands thee Be gone!

If they Roid still does not depart you must be forceful. You must invoke the opposing elementals to banish the Roid. Each Roid belongs to one element, you must invoke the other three to combat it. Know that the Anal Snake is of Water. Read the elements from East to North.

The power of <element 1> banishes you to the Kingdom
The power of <element 2> banishes you to the Kingdom
The power of <element 3> banishes you to the Kingdom
The word of Heme banishes you to the Kingdom The command of Gordon banishes you to the Kingdom

To Enlist the Help of KEEM IIST

As we get closer to the Third Coming, the chances of anal attack are increased.

If you are unfortunate to become a victim of the Roids then you can enlist the help of Keem Iist to fight back. Keem Iist is a descendant of the Keepers of the Cream, and still carries the secret ingredients for the sacred Balm: the cream of Ral Lief.

Firstly you must, by application of your own wit locate a sacred temple of worship. The temple should be traced by following the light of the glowing green cross. Thus begins your first pilgrimage.

By Gord's mercy may you soon find the temple of Keem

Iist.

Note that upon your arrival you may find other
worshippers at the shrine of Keem Iist. Keem Iist
advises on all matters and does not distinguish on
grounds of race or practised religion, therefore he
is always busy.

Wait your turn and when the altar is clear of
worshippers you may approach. The first step is to
establish the identity of the deity. Speak thus:

"Is this the sacred Keem Iist, provider of knowledge
and keeper of the sacred cooling balm, designed by
almighty Gord and provided to us mere mortals as the
cream of Ral Lief?"

On a positive response perform the greeting of Ral
Lief. Grab your buttocks with both hands, thus
causing separation within, spin around clockwise
three times and then jump-up twice. Look up at the
ceiling and declare in a loud voice thus:

"Ooooooooh Me Grapes". This will surely appease
Keem Iist and will solidify your claims for help.

Then declare thus, in a more moderate voice:

"Oh Great Keem Iist, holder of the Balm and adviser
on all things, including bad sexual encounters, I
implore thee for thy most Holy help. I have gazed
upon the Valley of the Scorched and I have observed
the gathering of the minions of Heme. I did this by
squatting above a large mirror. My Dark Cavern
glows red with fiery anger and I implore thee, oh
wise and most-merciful Keem Iist to provide me with
the sacred Balm, as given by Gord to his beloved
people, even the Dinosaurs though they did flaunt
the traits of greed and sexual deviances. I ask of
thee for a portion of the Balm, to be provided to me
encased in a Steele Gusset, and I ask for your great

wisdom regarding application of the cooling Balm. I must quench my anal fire and drive Heme back into the Dark Cavern, that is, back through the astral anchor located within my colon, at your wish. Init".

At this point Keem Iist will provide the sacred Balm in exchange for pieces of gold, silver and copper. He won't take frankincense or myrrh.

Keem Iist may try to give you more than the sacred Balm but politely refuse: for Keem Iist possesses wisdom of many things and is very fond of the gold, silver and copper trinkets.

Keem Iist has been known as a bit of a trickster: a loveable rogue. To put you off, Keem Iist make take the form of a woman, young and nubile, or old and with a moustache. Whatever form is taken, you may want to thank Keem Iist by performing the Dance of Heme (Book 3).

To Enlist the Help of DO TTHER

Consultation may also be sought with the wise and learned Do Tther, who shares an abode with Sir Gerry.

Many wise peoples have their own opinions on Do Tther and Sir Gerry's living arrangements. Some say they are both emanations of the same energy, others that Do Tther is a lesser vision granted by Sir Gerry. The accepted theory is that they are a bunch of raving homosexuals, and that that suites them just fine, since Sir Gerry always appears to be well insulated from noisy internal emanations.

To address Do Tther you must first locate the abode of Sir Gerry. It is rumoured that Sir Gerry is listed within the sacred book of Yellow, the tome of

non-deviant finger flicking: the Yol Oh Pa Jes.
However, magicians know this: it takes a certain
strength to successfully use the book of Yol Oh Pa
Jes, since it is rumoured to be a very heavy book.

On finding Sir Gerry, enter him and approach the
reception. Herein lies another mystery. If Sir
Gerry is a raving homosexual then why does he
appoint as his receptionists lusty women? It is
rumoured that the reception staff are Sir Gerry's
daughters, conceived by the government department
for sexual equality.

Never mind, approach these maidens and smile at
them.

Then you must drop your trousers, grasp your
buttocks (thus causing separation), turn around and
talk to them as if your very arse were pleading for
their mercy. The maidens are notoriously difficult:
for they are the guardians of Do Tther and make sure
he doesn't stray to another man, since Do Tther has
a reputation for putting it around a bit too much.

Speak thus from your vibrating cheeks:

"Help me, help me! See my affliction! I have Roid
plaque within the mouth of my Dark Cavern. They
must be extinguished! Oh they burn me! It is as if
I have eaten hot chilli, though I don't eat chilli,
I don't eat anything: I'm only meant to expel. I
need to see Do Tther. I promise Sir Gerry I will
not try anything with Do Tther: my condition is too
serious and my ding-dong is not worthy. See my
raspberry beard, see my red grapes hanging, see them
Glow. See them wink. I must have Ral Lief".

Then spin round three times, jump-up twice and,
cheeks spread far apart scream:

"Oooooooooooooooh, me grapes".

Rise, buckle-up your trousers once more, lean forward with a practised dignity and say in a low, sweet voice:

" I need help".

After this you would have certainly gained the respect of Sir Gerry's daughters, and they will surely usher you in to see their fathers blatant lover.

You may wish to thank the maidens by performing the Dance of Heme (Book 3).

"They move as per the cat amongst the pigeons. Alas a cat can be seen, and thus the pigeon has wings".
Joseph. 41.

Closer to God
By Joseph. 41

I've been sat at the window for a day and a half
now, staring, watching the evolved truths migrate
forthwards unto my understanding. For the window is
a ledger of truth, a gateway into truths beheld and
into truths sheathed.

Images blur into my mind from the surface of the
window, bypassing my vision though I know this
cannot be. I know not where to search, nor do I
know what I expect to find. But thus far my search
has been both compelling and revealing. Though the
images seen are blurred and nonsensical, they bring
forth understanding. I cannot explain it, though I
know I cannot stop; I sense my journey is almost at
a closure.

Time spurns onwards. I have lost count of the
hours, of the days I have sat here, staring into the
window. I have not moved for fear of losing my
path. I could not bear being unable to retrace my
steps, for I have journeyed so far; I have gained so
much understanding.

My body now weeps for sustenance, though I cannot, I
dare not leave the window. My mind strengthens with
each rising of the new sun, and with its every
closure. The images are getting more blurred now,
more surreal. Though my body is dying my mind feasts
veraciously, though now with more cryptic drippings.

I am ever closer to that which remains unknown.   To
the elusive nectar of all that shall not be
revealed.

I have seen it now. My sustained gaze upon the
window has brought forth the terrible truth of all

truths. That its image cannot be captured within a
thousand words gives justice to its grandeur yet
betrays its simplicity. The one. The father-truth.

That the truth could assume a different guise within
a different searching mind I am uncertain. But I
know. I have seen it, and I now understand. Staring
into the glassed-reflection of my eyes, into the
deepest recesses of my soul I have beheld that which
stares back. I understand. I understand but too
well...

The light of the world grows ever dimmer as the
blackness of space expands and the bleakness of time
marches onwards, unrepentant. My mind is tired of
its tenuous grip on inherited reality, and each
drawn breath of air is evermore punishable to my
lungs.

I shall be dead soon, that is certain. Then may my
efforts too, as those before me, be abdicated to the
window. To the window that killed me. To the window
I love. To the window that hangs on my wall, framed
in brass. Not a window to the outside, but a window
to the inside. A reflection into that which is
truly real; into that which is true. Do you not
know the secrets of your fellow man as you stare
past their eyes and confront their soul? Then search
for the ultimate truth, for your ultimate truth. As
I have done.

I shall pass contented.

For I know the truth.

LIBER 3 :: OF JOSEPH AND HIS MADNESS

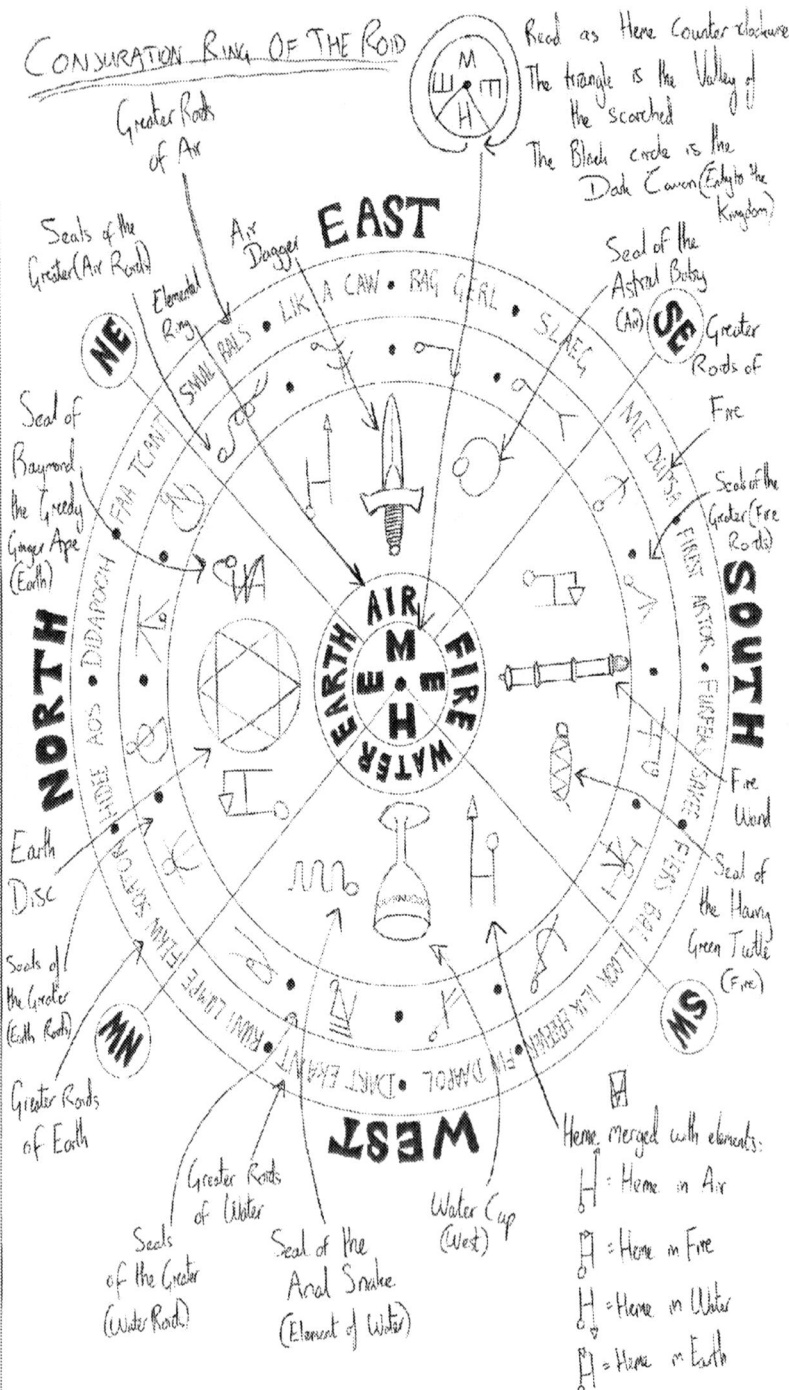

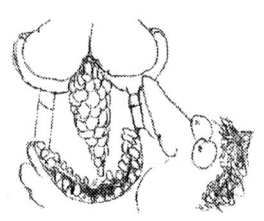

Be warned! These are not cute little Red berries but are daemons from the Abyss. Do not, at any point attempt to eat them. They will try and tempt you, oh they will try! By being Red. Be strong. Think of England.

~

They are nothing but Arse terrorists. Don't be suprised if you sufferers out there get a missile up your ass courtesy of Uncle SAM. The 'roids are tresspassing on your arse. If someone camped on your lawn in a big red tent you'd either move them yourself or ask the Police. To a 'roid, the 'police' are The keepers of the Cream.

METHOD FOR OVERCOMING TOMATO FETISH

It is hard to break off a relationship, especially one with a tomato. I have found a way. Take heed of my words. This ritual will cure your unholy lust for the forbidden fruit. IF it doesn't work immediately, try again.

THE RITUAL

Go to the Green Grocers or supermarket and select a single big, ripe tomato. DO NOT MAKE LOVE TO THIS TOMATO. Put it in a bag and put it in your pocket. Go to your local pub (or a pub in an appropriate locale) and stay there until closing, consuming as many beers as you see fit to do so. On your way home, stop at the first cow you come across. Take the tomato out of your pocket. Take the tomato out of the bag. Shove the tomato up the cow's arse yelling "Be gone, ye seductor of Heme" and leave a poster stuck onto the cow with sticky-tape thus;

A photograph of a local monkey is better but a picture will do. The V sign is a swear, not 'peace'.

THE MONKEY DID IT

The monkey is destined to rule Earth, so the more trouble we cause him the better.

When you transcend the 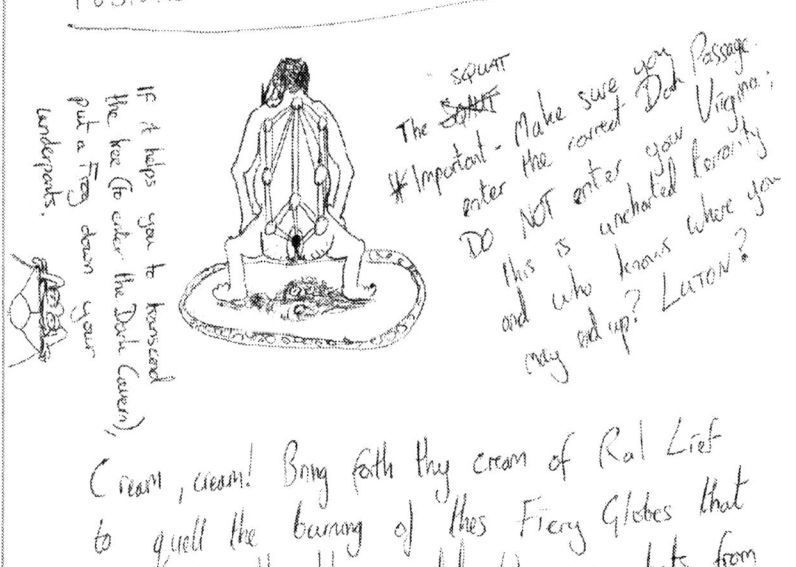 beware the wormholes within. These link together all of mankind and if you get sucked in, you may end-up emerging from someone else's arse-hole. This proves the fact that mankind is one big arse-hole. If you join up the possible wormholes it can be seen that the arsehole of mankind looks a bit like Wales, or George W Bush depending on your angle.

POSTURE TO TRANSCEND THE TREE

If it helps you to transcend the tree (ie enter the Dark Cavern), put a Frog down your underpants.

SQUAT
The ~~SHIT~~
*Important - Make sure you enter the correct Dark Passage. DO NOT enter your Virgina; this is uncharted teritory and who knows where you may end up? LUTON?

Cream, cream! Bring forth thy cream of Real Lief to quell the burning of thes Fiery Globes that doth hangeth like rounded Vampire bats from my hairy ring piece.

His name shall be Heme M and his pain shall
be the fiery-Rod. He cometh from the Red
cave of Fire, seated aloft his monstrous
Hairy Green Turtle. And his sustainance
shall be the wine of the grape. Not the
grape of the Vine but the grape of
the sinner. The Red grape. The
grape of the Arse.

~~

SPANKING THE MONKEY

SPANK THAT BASTARD
MONKEY UNTIL HE
CRIES, FOR HE IS
TO REIGN AT MANS
EXPENSE. IF YOU
CAN, GET A
FRIEND TO HELP

RITUAL TO BRING GOOD LUCK

On the third day of a month that contains the letter 'R', venture forth (after dark) and secure the services of a stray dog. Invite the dog back to your home for a game of poker. You must play three games of poker with this dog, of which you must win at least two. This task must be completed before the sun starts to rise.

If you win you will be afforded the luxury of the luck of kings.

If you loose, the dog has the right to demand of you a licking of his tiny bollsack.

IT is written that the great Hairy Green Turtle
will carry  from the darkside of the Abyss
into the light. Then shall be realised
and then shall he call to his minions.
Prepare the cream of Ral Lief: The
eternal stance of the gape is upon us.

CAMUEL, WITHIN THE PLANE OF FIRE

The Garden of Eden? My Arse

Like Red hot Stalactites they hang within the great Cavern of My Arse, mocking me. Bring forth my Shears, so that I may chop these fiends from my Seat.

Oh Tomato, how lustful... (surrounding text around the tomato face, partly illegible)

— Self portrait

— Joseph aged 4!

(vertical text, left side)
Let me unleash my grapes of wrath and even the almighty shall tremble, for there shall be no sitting down and these cliff become very tired in their eternal stare.

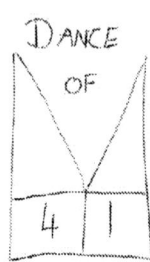

DANCE OF

| 4 | 1 |

"Be at one with Sandy Tocksvig, and dance like a bitch to please your master"

E

1.

2.

3.

4.

5.

6.

7.

You must perform
E,S,W,N

8.

THE LEAP OF FAITH

170

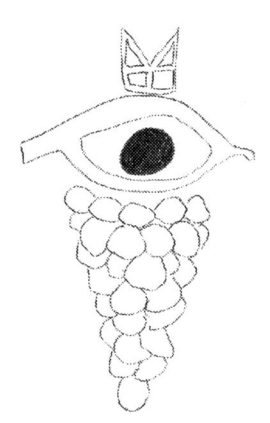

THE LEFT EYE OF HEME WATCHES US ALWAYS, EVER STARING, EVER BLACK. HE WAITS, AS HE HAS WAITED FOR OVER TWO THOUSAND YEARS. BUT NOW THE TIME COMES. MAN IS APPROACHING THE ABYSS AND THERE SHALL BE NO TURNING BACK AND THERE SHALL BE NO EXCEPTIONS. THE KINGDOM SHALL LIVE AGAIN!   HAIL THE ROIDS
                HAIL TO HEME

WE WILL ALL BURN

- JOSEPH, 41

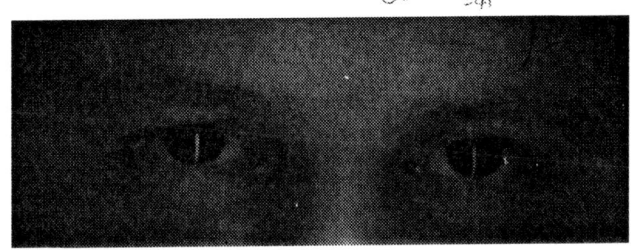

171

When you look what do you see
The years bittersweet, laying upon me?
Do you see hate, despair?
Lonesome with solitude, or a sunken glare?
Which is it for you?

That which is shall always be
And in our darkness shall set us free.
No shining light for me.
Just blackness.

Look upon the eyes of man with caution
For you look into the eyes of your
destroyer.
Dollar-ideals awash with our blood.
Are you afraid?

I am.
For I am Truth.